Leye Adenle is a Nigerian-born crime writer, known for his gripping stories that explore human nature's dark side. His debut novel, *Easy Motion Tourist*, won the prestigious Prix Marianne in France in 2016, and in 2024 he was awarded the Lawrence Prize for his short story *The House of Oluawo*. As one of the most exciting voices in contemporary crime fiction, Adenle's writing is characterised by vivid, gritty descriptions of Nigerian society, capturing the complexity of a country often misunderstood by outsiders . . .

Also by Leye Adenle

THE AMAKA THRILLERS
Easy Motion Tourist
When Trouble Sleeps
Unfinished Business

STANDALONE NOVELS
The Beautiful Side of the Moon

CELL ONE

LEYE ADENLE

**SIMON &
SCHUSTER**

London · New York · Amsterdam/Antwerp · Sydney/Melbourne · Toronto · New Delhi

Chapter 1

He groaned. His head throbbed. The pain was sickening. It was the worst hangover ever. He should not have drunk so much at the party.

He couldn't move. It was like one of those dreams where your mind wakes up but your body continues to sleep. He tried again. Something wasn't right. Then, he realised. His hands and feet were bound. Panic.

He opened his eyes. Pitch darkness. Absolute silence. The only thing he could hear was the sound of his own breathing as he tried to free himself.

What was happening?

His heart pounded. His head hurt. He had to get free. He summoned all his strength, but he couldn't break loose. He realised that he was naked, tied to a chair with what felt like zip ties and trapped in a dark room. The ties bit into his wrists behind his back and into his ankles. Was this a joke?

His heart pounded faster.

He moved his feet and searched with his toes. The floor was smooth, cold and rubbery. He tried to rock the chair. It didn't move.

He stopped. He sat still and listened. His heart beat so hard that he felt it in his neck. The silence filled him with terror.

'Help!' he shouted. 'Help!'

It sounded like he was screaming into a well.

He kept yelling and trying to free himself until he was out of breath.

Panting in that total darkness, he tried to think. He couldn't remember anything. He didn't know where he was, how he'd got there, when he'd got there or who had taken him there.

Warm urine ran down the inside of his thigh and down his calf. His body shook with terror. He had been kidnapped.

He must have blacked out again. When he came to, for a moment he didn't remember where he was. He blinked and blinked, but he couldn't blink the blindness away. Then he remembered; he could feel the plastic ties around his wrists and ankles, and he began to whimper in the darkness. Tears fell from his eyes as he whispered the Lord's prayer.

'Our Father, who art in heaven . . .'

Two blinding lights hummed to life a few feet in front of him. His heart leapt. The brilliance burned his eyes. He shut them and twisted away, but the light burned through his eyelids. His heart pumped, threatening to explode. He could hear himself panting. His chest heaved, and he clenched his fists behind his back as he waited for whatever was to come.

It was dark beyond the lamps that hummed in the silence of his prison. He couldn't look directly at the lights, but he could see around him now.

The metal chair was blue. The last time he had seen one like it was at parties when he was in his teens. Leaning to one side, he could see square plates beneath each leg, under the black rubber that covered the floor. Whoever had imprisoned him here had welded the chairs to the ground. The rubber continued up the walls. He looked up. A thin tube stretched down behind him from a dark hole the size of a football above his head. Arching his head as far back as he could, he traced the line to a needle in his left arm. He saw the clear fluid in it.

'Hey!'

He yelled in panic and rocked himself in the chair.

He screamed at the lights, dodging their beams, trying to see who stood in the shadows behind them.

'Hey! Who are you? What do you want from me?'

He listened. His breaths were short and fast. He readied himself.

But no one answered him.

The lights flicked off, and silence returned. As the bright after-image faded, total darkness settled once more.

When he woke up again, he began to cry.

He sobbed like he hadn't done in years. Tears fell freely from his eyes. Mucus ran down from his nostrils. He cried into the darkness until he couldn't cry anymore.

He had no idea how long he had been there. Hours? Days?

He longed for the lights to switch on again. Who were they? What did they want? What were they putting into his body through the tube?

He let his head slump down. His chin rested on his chest. He stared at memories in the darkness. His wife. His three girls – the first had just graduated from law school; the twins were at boarding school in the East. Their mother had been apprehensive over sending them so far away from home. Nigeria wasn't what it used to be.

Then a fearful thought entered his mind – even more terrifying than being kidnapped for ransom. What if the people who had him were ritualists?

His bowels let go. Fear gripped his chest. He panted 'Jesu' with each exhale. Each breath felt like the end.

The lights turned on. The beams were warm on his skin.

He spoke quickly. 'I am not rich,' he shouted. 'But my wife has money. There is up to fifty million naira in her business account. If you let me talk to her, I will convince her to hand over all the money in exchange for me. Please. That is all the money we have. Just let me talk to her. Please. I beg you, in the name of God.

'I have not seen your face. I do not know who you are. We will give you all the money, plus everything I have in my own account. Please. Have mercy on us, in God's name, please!'

A speaker crackled to life in the darkness that remained behind the floodlights.

An electronic voice spoke:

'The wages of sin is death. Confess your sin, and you shall be free.'

'I beg you, in the name of God!' he shouted back. 'Whatever you want, we will give you! Please, just let me talk to my wife.'

There was a rustling sound above. He looked up. Water began to gush down from the hole over his head.

He tried to scream, but the cold water suffocated him as the torrent continued. No matter how he moved his head, he couldn't avoid it. If it didn't stop, he would die.

The water stopped.

Exhausted and trembling, he desperately gulped down air in gasps. His heart raced uncontrollably. He looked down. His feet were submerged in water up to his calves.

The lights went off. He shivered in the dark.

Chapter 2

'Good morning. My name is Bobby. Bobby Fatokun. The director of SCIID in Panti gave me this letter for you.'

It was my third week in Nigeria after receiving a letter in the UK congratulating me on my new job as an Assistant Superintendent of Police in the Cybercrime Unit of the Nigerian Police Force. I'd been stunned when I'd opened it. The Nigerian police had been recruiting at a fair in London, but never in a thousand years did I think my application would result in a call-up letter. Now I should have been in my second week of training at the Police Academy, but instead here I was, reporting to a police station that wasn't expecting me.

Superintendent of Police Balogun didn't look up from the documents on his desk as he held out his hand for the letter.

After he finished reading, he turned it over to see if there was more of an explanation for why I was at his station. He looked up at me doing my best to stand to attention in front of his desk at the Bar Beach Police Station, Victoria Island, Lagos.

I didn't yet have my uniform, so I was in a white dress shirt tucked into a pair of dark blue chinos, and I was wearing the only pair of smart shoes I'd brought with me from England. The irregular humming and occasional clanking of the air conditioner kept me wondering if it was safe to have it on, but I was grateful for the cooler air in his office. I was still getting used to the intense heat in Nigeria. I didn't remember it being so hot when I left as a child.

Balogun measured me with his eyes, no doubt wondering why I had turned up dressed as a civilian.

'What exactly am I to do with you?' he asked.

I didn't know the answer, and I didn't know if he expected me to.

I'd reported to the SCIID, the State Criminal Investigation and Intelligence Department in Panti, as instructed, and there the issues had started.

The force had cancelled the international recruitment drive that had resulted in my hiring. There was no further explanation provided. I was, however, still owed a position, but not at the rate in my contract, and the vacancy in the cybercrime unit no longer existed, at least not for now. My best option, they told me, was to visit the police headquarters in Abuja; perhaps someone there could assist me. After a week in Abuja, an equally confused Commissioner of Police finally gave me a letter to take to Bar Beach Police Station. 'They have a cybercrime unit,' he said. 'Maybe they'll have something for you to do in the meantime.'

'In the meantime' meant 'Until we know what to do with you.' Or 'It is their problem now.' And indeed, SP Balogun looked at me as if I was a problem that he could do without.

'It says here that you were recruited from England.'

It was a statement. I didn't know if he meant it as a question. One thing I'd learned while seeking help at headquarters was to remain silent until a senior officer asked a question.

Another lesson I'd learned was that my London accent either fascinated or irritated others. There was no in-between. An officer I'd encountered at headquarters had rubbed his head as I spoke before asking me to 'Speak normal English.' As a result, I quickly mastered the art of switching accents, but my genuine accent still sometimes surfaced, giving me away.

I had used my best Nigerian English with

SP Balogun, but I could see that he wasn't buying it.

'I didn't even know they were recruiting from abroad,' he said. 'Who arranged the appointment for you?'

I didn't know what he meant, so I kept quiet.

'Who is your godfather?'

'I don't have a godfather.'

'Really? I won't find out that the Inspector General is your uncle?'

I smiled as I shook my head. But he wasn't joking.

'We don't normally recruit from abroad,' he went on. 'And I see that you have joined with the rank of Deputy Superintendent of Police. That is just one rank below me. It is high for someone without any police training. Who helped you secure the appointment?'

I stood up taller. 'Nobody did. There was a job fair in London, and I applied.'

'Are you telling me that you don't know anybody in the system? Who spoke to the recruiters on your behalf?'

'Nobody. The role sounded good, and I applied.'

'And they just gave you a job.' He looked unconvinced.

'They wanted people with advanced

qualifications or experience in cybercrime. I had just finished my Master's in IT. I wrote my thesis on cybercrime.'

'I see. How long have you been out of Nigeria?'

'Since I was a child.'

'And you never came back?'

'No.'

Balogun sighed. 'Okay. First lesson. When you are talking to a senior officer, you say "Sir", okay?'

'Okay.'

He shook his head. 'No. Not okay. Try again.'

'Okay, sir.'

A phone rang on his table. He had three next to each other, all of them in different colours.

He continued to inspect my appearance as he took the call. It was obvious he didn't want me there any more than I did. Working in a small police station was not what I had signed up for. I imagined sharing my problem with my mother. She would definitely say, 'I told you so,' then she would offer to send me a ticket for the first flight back to London.

'Why is she asking for me?' Balogun said to the person calling him.

His face was even more contorted than it had been when he'd read my letter. He now looked visibly annoyed. It didn't bode well for me.

'Okay, put her through.'

While he waited for the call to be connected, he looked at me once again. His stare travelled from my head down as far as he could see from behind his desk and back up. Each time, he managed to just miss my eyes. Perhaps he was looking for a reason to send me away. After all, I didn't have a 'Godfather,' as he had described it, to protect me.

'Good morning, Madam.' His entire demeanour changed. Smiling for the sake of the person on the phone, even his voice had turned meek. He stared at my letter on his desk as he listened to the caller.

'Me? I left long before the party ended. Maybe he was tired, and he decided to spend the night at the mess . . . Alright, Ma. I will send someone to go and check . . . Yes, Ma, I have his number . . . Maybe his battery died . . . Yes, Ma. Right away, Ma . . . No, Ma. I don't think there is any need to panic . . . Okay, Ma.'

He replaced the handset and shook his head. He picked up one of the other phones and spoke into it. 'Send Abike.'

Picking his mobile off the desk, he sat back to make another call. Someone knocked on the door while he still had the phone pressed to his ear. A moment later, the person walked in.

It was a female officer. She stood next to me and briefly checked me out.

She was my height in her black combat boots. Her skin was dark like that of a Sudanese model, and she had a no-nonsense face that could have advertised beauty products on a billboard. I wouldn't have had the guts to talk to her at a party.

He placed the phone down. 'You won't believe it. Oga Adams didn't go home yesterday,' he said.

The woman snorted as if it was to be expected. Balogun had referred to Adams as 'Oga', meaning 'boss', so I assumed he was their superior.

'I think he left with that girl he was drinking with,' Balogun added. 'His wife just called me. She said he wasn't answering his phone this morning, then he switched it off around seven. It's still off.'

'Maybe his battery died,' Abike said. 'Mariam and I left late but his car was still in the car park at the officers' mess. Maybe he stayed over.'

'Again?' Balogun shook his head and lowered his mobile. 'This man. I just tried to call the place, but no one is answering. Please, go and find him before his wife gets there.'

'Maybe we should let her catch him. That girl could not have been older than his daughter.'

'Oga Adams,' Balogun said, shaking his head. 'Something must kill a man.'

Indeed, I thought. Everyone has a weakness and a man will chase it, come what may.

He seemed to remember I was there. 'This is ASP Fatokun,' he said. Abike looked me up and down again in light of the new information. 'Headquarters sent him this morning. He will be working with you and Rocky. Take him with you.'

Chapter 3

I followed Abike through the station, drawing stares as I tried to keep up with her.

I started sweating as soon as we stepped outside. I hoped that her car had air-conditioning. It didn't. The driver of the patrol vehicle, a sergeant named Sule, gave me a questioning look as I climbed in before Abike. He seemed surprised when I held my hand out. He dusted roasted peanut skins off his palms and lap before taking it.

As we drove out of the station, I held my hand out to Abike and said, 'Hi, I'm Bobby,' just as she asked, 'Where did you transfer from?'

'I'm new,' I said. 'I'm just starting today.'

'You sound like someone from abroad.'

'I just relocated from England.'

'England? And you came to Nigeria to work for the police?'

I was used to this – the disbelief when people learned that I had relocated from England to join the Nigerian Police Force. Had I been a Premier League footballer who'd abandoned the Three Lions to play for Nigeria, I would have been praised for my loyalty, but instead I was regarded with suspicion. Even Sule gave me a second look.

'I did my Master's in IT and wrote my dissertation on cybercrime,' I said. 'I was meant to join the cybercrime unit at Panti, but I guess someone there didn't get the memo.'

'And so they dumped you on us,' she said. She made no attempt to hide her contempt. Or was it indifference?

'Rocky and I run our own little cybercrime outfit here,' she continued. 'We work with Panti on big cases if we need their help, but so far, we've mostly been able to do without them. Our unit is still young, but if it works, it will serve as a model for other stations. So, I guess we can use you. Rocky is our in-house computer specialist. I'm sure he'll be glad to meet you. I hope you have your own laptop.'

'I do.'

I wanted to say that using my own laptop at work was breaking the first rule of cybersecurity, but I kept quiet for now.

'Good. And try to turn up in uniform tomorrow.'

'How do I get one?' I asked. 'Do I need to fill out a form?'

Both she and Sule looked at me.

'You have to sew your own,' she said.

For a moment I thought she was joking.

The Police Officers' Mess at Onikan was a short drive from the station. I had been offered a room in the hotel there, but my mother, ever wary, had instead secured a suite for me at a place her friend suggested – Ten Rooms, a boutique hotel with an outdoor terrace overlooking the lagoon. Seeing the officers' mess for the first time, I was glad I wasn't staying there. The complex was run-down, just like the police station, with paint peeling off the buildings and weeds growing from the corners of the driveway.

Adams' car was alone in a section of the parking lot close to the gate – a black Honda with worn tyres. I looked around for cameras. There were none. Abike and I headed for the bar, where she told me her colleagues had been celebrating Adams' promotion the night before.

The space smelled of stale beer and lingering tobacco smoke. It was dark inside, owing to the thick drapes over the windows. A handful of officers sat in pairs, bent over in conversation. A muted TV on the wall was tuned to CNN. We went straight to the bar, where a man in a chef's hat and a woman in a white shirt and black trousers were talking. They both knew Abike and they both gave me the once over. Both of them were aware that Adams' car had spent the night in the car park after the party. Neither of them remembered who he had left with. The chef was confident that Adams hadn't spent the night at the hotel.

'They usually tell the kitchen when new guests are staying,' he explained. 'I haven't received any notification. We currently have only four occupied rooms, all booked since Friday.'

Still, we visited the front desk, where a slim young man confirmed this. Abike asked to see the register, and then we visited each of the four occupied suites and she questioned the guests. None of them knew anything about Adams.

Outside in the car park, I followed her over to the black Honda. She tried the doors, setting off the alarm. As it blared hysterically, we looked through the windows at the inside.

'Can you track phones?' I asked.

'What kind of question is that?'

She fetched her mobile, then paused, staring at the device, before looking up at me.

'Listen,' she said. 'You have to get rid of that accent; otherwise, people will take advantage of you. After we sort this out, I'll take you to buy your materials, and then we'll go to a tailor. Let me do all the talking if you don't want to pay double.'

She really hadn't been joking when she'd said I had to sew my own uniform. And apparently, it wasn't just that. I was also expected to buy my own boots, regulation berets, tear gas, torches, whistles, handcuffs and batons. Thank God I didn't need most of those, but even so, it was a shock. Though if the mix-up with my appointment hadn't fazed me, shelling out a few pounds for my uniform wouldn't break me either.

'Aren't you worried that Adams is missing?' I asked while she dialled.

When I'd told my mother about the job offer with the Nigerian police, she'd reminded me that the country had become notorious for kidnappings since we'd left.

'What good would worrying do?' Abike asked.

She made her call and put the phone on speaker for my sake. Balogun answered on the first ring.

'Talk to me,' he said.

'Oga, he's not here,' Abike said.

'His phone last pinged a tower in Kogi,' Balogun said. 'Felix and his team are taking the chopper.'

'Has there been a ransom call?' Abike asked.

'No. And it's very important to keep this quiet until we know what's going on. I need you to go to his house and stay with his wife in case anyone calls. And make sure she doesn't talk to anyone. Call me when you get there. Is Fatokun there?'

She looked at me.

I bent towards the phone in her palm. 'I'm here,' I said. I cursed under my breath and quickly added, 'I'm here, sir.'

'Do whatever Abike tells you to do, okay?'

'Yes, sir.' I saw a chance to impress both of them – I took it. 'I was thinking, sir. Since it was his party, people must have been taking pictures. If we contact the guests and ask for the pictures they took, we might find something useful.'

He didn't respond. Abike looked at me. Their silence convinced me that I shouldn't have spoken.

'Call me when you get there,' Balogun said, and ended the call.

*

Adams' home was in a place called Gbagada. It was at least an hour's drive. It would have been more, but Sule intermittently activated his siren to get us through the notorious Lagos traffic. He even used the hard shoulder once, which made me anxious until I remembered that we were the police.

I was quiet while we drove, remembering my conversation with Abike before we'd left.

'Listen,' she'd said as we'd walked to the van. 'Stop talking unless someone asks for your opinion. The problem with people like you is that you think you're better than locals because you studied abroad. Look, we're not stupid here. Lose that know-it-all attitude before you irritate everybody.'

Her words stung, but she was right. What was I thinking? I was new – what did I know? And to make things worse, nobody wanted me there.

'Sure,' I said.

She stopped abruptly.

'You really don't get it, do you?' she said. 'All of us worked hard for this. We trained hard, we drilled hard and we studied hard. We cut our teeth in the field. But you: someone made a call, and now you're here living out a police-and-thief fantasy. This is not a game. People lose their lives in this job. Those men going to Kogi to look for Adams – if he has been kidnapped, some of them might not come back. Do you understand? This is not a game, so stop trying to impress anyone. You're just exposing your ignorance.'

Now her voice jolted me out of my daze.

'We're here.'

Sule roared to a stop and we got out.

We were parked outside a well-to-do estate. The neighbourhood was quiet until the instant Abike knocked on the gate. Dogs started barking and an Alsatian poked its snout out of the space between the gate and the fence, snarling and baring its teeth. I froze.

A scrawny young man in a white singlet and flowery shorts appeared and invited us inside while we waited for Adams' wife to walk down from her shop. It was less than ten minutes away, he assured us. Abike thanked him and said that we would wait in the van. I was so relieved.

'She doesn't seem that bothered,' I said.

Sule started the engine and turned the AC back on when we climbed back inside.

Abike didn't look up from her phone. She had been reading and sending messages since we left the station. She paused mid-message and looked up at me, her thumbs hovering over the screen.

She looked straight into my eyes. She didn't talk. Her lips twitched ever so slightly.

She turned back to her phone and continued typing.

I realised that I'd just shared my opinion again without being asked for it.

'We told her to go to the shop this morning, as usual,' she said, still typing. 'There's a protocol when an officer is kidnapped. It's about maintaining normal patterns; no sudden changes, no panic. If they're watching, they must think we don't know.'

She looked up at me again. This time, I could tell she wasn't thinking of what to type. She tilted her face to one side, as if another angle would help. She bit her lip and I knew she was deciding whether to tell me. She knew something.

A slender woman with grey undergrowth beneath her cornrows tapped on the van's bonnet as she walked up to the gate. A policeman casually holding an assault rifle by his side walked a few paces behind her. I noticed how he kept looking around as he walked.

Abike started and put the phone away.

Without a word, we got out of the van and followed them.

I finally got my first look at Adams in the top-floor flat of a three-storey building in the gated estate. A life-size picture of him and his wife on their wedding day greeted me as I entered their living room.

Abike introduced me. We all sat in oversized cream leather chairs. I remained silent, allowing her to speak while I took in the surroundings. There were family photos everywhere, but none of the children seemed to be around. It was deathly silent, as if the house itself awaited bad news.

'Were you also at the party yesterday?' the lady asked Abike.

I couldn't tell if she was worried. I imagined that the police would have informed her if they were certain of her husband's kidnapping. I suspected that I was the only one who remained in the dark. She wore a stern look, sat perfectly still, and her speech was calm and measured. Was she in shock?

'I was there,' Abike said.

'Who was with him?'

'We were all there.'

'Abike, don't. Who did he bring?'

'I don't know her, Ireti.'

The woman abruptly stood up and began searching her body and looking around. She found her phone on a stool next to her. She scrolled through it and held the screen out to Abike. It was a social media profile picture.

'Is this her?'

Abike remained silent.

'Is it?'

Abike nodded.

'Her name is Bolanle Solarin. She goes by Suzie. Law student at Unilag. I only just found out about this one last month.'

She sounded matter-of-fact, as if she were merely dealing with a routine process and not the possible kidnapping of her unfaithful husband.

'She lives in Festac. I'm sending you her address and her phone number.'

Abike's phone beeped. She checked the message. 'How did you get this information?' she asked.

'Does it matter? Let's go and ask her what she did with him.'

'Ireti, please, sit down.'

'Don't tell me to sit down. Why are you still sitting down? Let's go.'

Abike looked uncomfortable. 'My colleagues

already took her in for questioning this morning. She's not involved.'

'Okay. Take me to the station. I want to hear her tell me herself.'

'Ireti, you know we can't do that. And you cannot go to her house. Please tell me you won't.'

'If he's been kidnapped . . .'

'We don't know that yet.'

'As I was saying. If he's been kidnapped, maybe she planned it.'

The young man who'd let us in had entered the room. He stood by the door.

'What is it?' Ireti asked him.

'Madam, there is something.'

'What?'

'Mariam showed me on her phone. It's about Oga.'

Abike was up in a flash. I followed suit.

'What is it?' Ireti asked him.

'It's on Natasha Gist Blog, Ma.'

Both women started working their phones.

'What is this?' Ireti said, looking at her screen.

I was still searching for the blog. Abike made a phone call.

'Hello, sir . . . Yes, sir . . . We are still there . . . No call yet. Sir, there's something you have to see. I just sent you a link.'

Abike was typing furiously. Ireti looked frazzled for the first time. She kept tapping on her screen, a confounded look on her face.

Abike looked up. 'Where are the children?'

'They're with my sister,' Ireti said. 'I followed the protocol.'

Abike continued with her message.

I was totally lost.

As their conversation faded into the background, I clicked on a search result and finally ended up on what should be the blog's home page.

I had to double-check the URL. The entire page was filled with a headshot of Chief Superintendent of Police Adams. He was in ceremonial uniform. His full name and rank were above the picture, in a large red font against a black background. Beneath the picture, '12:00 West African Time' flashed in red, and beneath that, a timer counted down to noon. What was happening?

I double-checked my watch. Whatever it was, there were less than fifteen minutes to go.

Chapter 4

An exposé. It had to be. Something big was going to be revealed about Adams. I looked at his wife. She was staring at her phone. Her face was squashed with confusion. I felt bad for her. Her missing, cheating husband was probably in hiding. He knew what was coming, and he'd bailed rather than face public disgrace or arrest.

'Do you have a computer we can use?' Abike asked Ireti.

Ireti turned to the young man. 'Go and bring my laptop.'

Her phone rang just as the young man left. We all stared at it. Abike and I watched as Ireti picked it up. I held my breath. It could be Adams calling from hiding – perhaps to prepare her for the news. Or to offer an explanation he'd been crafting. A desperate lie. What was the world going to learn about him at noon?

Ireti rejected the call.

'It's my sister,' she said.

The phone began to ring again. It was still in her hand.

'My pastor,' she said, looking frustrated. She let the phone ring.

'You need to keep the line clear,' Abike reminded her.

Ireti nodded and rejected the call. Her calm was beginning to show signs of cracking. Her brow crinkled, her lips twitching with words she couldn't say. Every now and then she shook her head. It was heartbreaking to watch.

The phone began to ring again. Then to beep with incoming messages. Abike's also started vibrating and beeping.

I checked the countdown on my screen: ten minutes till noon.

'What will happen at noon?' Ireti asked no one in particular.

It was the question on all our minds – and, I suspected, on the minds of the people who kept calling her and sending messages.

I took another look at the website. On closer inspection, it appeared to have been hacked. Google informed me that it was Nigeria's top-ranking blog, receiving millions of international views per day. Those millions of people were all waiting for noon.

'Ireti,' Abike said, 'whatever it is, don't let it get to you. Give me your phone.'

The phone kept ringing and beeping, and Ireti kept rejecting the calls. She handed it to Abike. She looked more confused than alarmed. She shook her head and kissed her teeth.

'This man has finally disgraced himself,' she said, her face contorted with pity and disappointment.

I was thinking the same. I just knew that something lurid was going to be revealed – I dared not imagine the details. All I knew was that it was so bad that he had gone into hiding. A Yoruba saying suddenly felt real: Death is better than disgrace. Oh dear.

The young man returned, panting. Ireti set the laptop on the table and opened up the morbid countdown. I thought I saw her hand tremble. I felt really bad for her. Abike moved to the sofa and held Ireti's hand while checking and rejecting calls on the poor woman's phone. Two minutes to go.

I watched Ireti. Her life was about to change forever. While I and everyone else watching the hacked website waited eagerly for the big reveal, I could only imagine how dreadful it felt for her. Fifty-nine seconds to go.

Forty seconds.

Twenty.

Ten.

Ireti's face scrunched up further with each moment that ticked by.

The screen turned black. I heard the rasp of her sharp inhale. In the bottom-right corner, a white timestamp appeared and glowed faintly. It was live.

My heart was beating with anticipation. I glanced at Ireti. Her lips were taut, her eyes were wide and unblinking, and her chest heaved with quick, short breaths. I felt so sorry for her.

Bright white light suddenly flooded the screen.

Abike gasped. Ireti screamed. She jumped out of her seat. The young man standing behind the sofa shouted, 'Jesus!' and held the crown of his head in his hands.

In an apparently windowless room with black walls, Chief Superintendent of Police Adams was bound to a chair, naked and wet. He raised his head and squinted at the bright light. He looked exhausted as he struggled to look past the beam.

The image was angled downwards. The ceiling wasn't visible. A thin, transparent line ran up from the back of the chair where Adams' arms were tied. Water shimmered midway up his legs.

'Jesus, Jesus, Jesus,' Ireti kept calling as she watched her husband on the screen of her computer.

Abike stood and tried to comfort her.

Adams spoke. He sounded weak. 'Please, I'm begging you. Let me go.'

Ireti pulled at her cornrows, stamping each foot on the ground in turn.

'It will be okay,' Abike said, her voice hoarse.

I doubted it.

Adams continued pleading for his life. Then his captor responded, their voice electronically altered:

'The wages of sin is death. Confess your sin, and you shall be free.'

'My enemies have won!' Ireti yelled, throwing her arms up, looking to the heavens. She started to fall backwards. Abike and the young man caught her and guided her gently onto the sofa. Abike held her hand. I couldn't begin to imagine how she felt.

Adam was struggling to keep his head up. It slumped forward and rolled to one side, before he looked up again, his face mangled with pain, sadness and frustration.

The voice repeated its warning message:

'The wages of sin is death. Confess your sin, and you shall be free.'

'Why are you doing this?' Adams asked, almost crying. 'Who are you people? What do you want?'

I noted that he'd said, 'People.' There was more than one abductor. Also, he didn't know who they were. I felt a tingle of excitement. I was thinking like a police officer.

Adams turned his head up and yelled, 'Help!'

I saw the pain register on Ireti's face. She twisted her hands together in anxiety.

Her phone rang. Abike looked at the screen. She rejected the call.

'Help!' Adams continued to scream loudly until he exhausted himself. He cocked one ear to the side and sat still for a moment. We watched as he glanced up, then tucked his chin into his chest and seemed to brace himself for something.

Suddenly a torrent of water began crashing down onto him. He screamed and rocked in the chair, trying to free himself. The water kept running. Adams gasped. He was suffocating.

I glanced at Ireti. Abike and the young man were holding her back. Her face was frozen in horror and pain. Her eyes were fixed on the screen, as though she couldn't bear to watch, but couldn't not watch. And her mouth was wide open in a silent, constant scream.

The water stopped just as suddenly as it had started. It had lasted about a minute. The level had risen to his knees. They were torturing him on a live broadcast! They meant to drown him!

The floodlights went off. The timestamp kept ticking. Adams' exhausted, laboured breaths were moments apart. They were harrowing to listen to.

The screen abruptly changed to the blog's homepage, and I became conscious of my own pounding heart.

Chapter 5

Abike took charge. She was taking calls, making calls and texting, while at the same time doing her best to soothe Ireti. All she had was me, a rookie on his first day with no training, no experience and no idea of what to do.

She looked at me. I could tell she was trying to remember my name.

'Bobby,' I said.

'Can you man the gate?'

If I'd been self-conscious about my lack of training before arriving at the flat, after watching the live feed, I now felt inadequate, unsafe and useless. I was grateful to have some responsibility.

The young man followed me downstairs. The officer who'd accompanied Ireti was outside the gate when we arrived. I read his name off his name badge. A K Idowu.

'Hi,' I said, holding out my hand. 'I'm ASP Fatokun.'

He saluted first, then accepted my handshake with a slight bow. My first salute.

Within minutes, cars were pulling up in front of the estate. Some paused at the gate, hoping to gain entry. Others found spaces to park along the road where neighbours were gathering, keeping vigil on the house. Some came over to us. I turned everyone away. Ireti didn't want to see anyone.

A minivan pulled up. The driver was a woman who bore a striking resemblance to Ireti. She came with her four children – Ireti's children – and her husband, a man with silver clips in his dreadlocks. The young man was already opening the gate. He waved as they drove in.

Uncles, aunties and all manner of relatives and friends of the family who lived close enough turned up. I thanked them on Ireti's behalf and firmly turned them back. No one objected even though I was in plain clothes. I must confess: authority felt good. I felt powerful.

I scanned the crowd, making sure to take in every single person as they arrived. I held my phone by my side, its camera pointing at them, capturing everyone as Abike had instructed before I'd come down. They were standing in groups, talking and taking pictures of the building. Within a few minutes, I was sure I could describe everyone if I had to. I'd even made eye contact with some of them. Then I noticed a man get off a motorcycle and pay the driver. The man pulled his black hooded top low over his face. He was light-skinned and wearing a pair of black sunshades as well as the hoodie.

The bike turned around and left. The man tucked his hands into the pockets of his hoodie. He walked along the road, stepped over the open gutter, stood on the pavement and looked up at the house.

He was behind a group of young girls. They were sitting on the edge of the pavement, with their legs over the gutter, talking. They paid him no notice.

I aimed the lens of my camera at him.

I was sweating under the hot sun, but his arms and head were covered by his black hoodie, leaving only part of his face visible.

Something about him made me uncomfortable. Was it the hoodie or the fact that he was alone?

A TV station's van arrived. Abike had given me a line to give them. As the reporters stepped out with their cameras and boom mike, I returned my attention to the man in the hoodie. Even though I couldn't see his eyes, I could tell from the tilt of his head that he was looking at the top floor of the building. He knew where the abducted CSP lived.

The news crew set up right in the middle of the road. I was dividing my attention between them and the man. Approaching sirens caught everyone's attention. Two police vans swept in, forcing people off the road and parking across it on either side of the gate. SP Balogun got out of one of them and began to walk towards the house as armed officers alighted and took up positions on the road. His name wasn't on the list. Ireti had specifically stated that she did not want to see any of Adams' friends. She meant her husband's colleagues, who had been at the now-infamous party.

As Balogun walked towards me, walkie-talkie in hand, I glanced briefly at the hooded man. His hands were in his pockets, his face fixed on Adams' home, but there was still something about him that made me feel uneasy.

'Fatokun,' Balogun said as he arrived. The officer with me saluted. I did my best to imitate it.

Balogun turned to scan the crowd. I looked for the black hoodie again. There he was, walking towards the estate gate up the road.

'Have you seen anything unusual?' Balogun asked.

Maybe the man in the hoodie was friends with the older daughter. Maybe that was how he knew the house. I remembered how Abike had told me not to embarrass myself.

'No, sir,' I said.

'How is Ireti?' he asked.

'She's quite distressed. She said she only wants her family around her right now.'

I hoped he got the gist.

Balogun nodded at the news crew. 'They've spotted me,' he said. The crew were looking at us. 'Let's go inside,' he went on. 'I don't have anything for them yet.'

The young man at the gate knew him. He shut it behind us.

'So, tell me, what do you think?' Balogun said as we walked.

'I don't know what to think, sir.'

I instantly felt stupid for admitting the truth. I had many questions, like, how exactly was Adams kidnapped from a party at the Police Officers' Mess? Was his girlfriend involved? Did Balogun know what sin the abductors were referring to?

'You know,' Balogun said, 'ever since this kidnapping thing took hold in the country, we've developed intelligence networks. Our snitches in the business have no idea who did this. They've been contacting us themselves. Imagine that? Kidnappers have been calling the police to say, "I had no hand in this, o!"'

I looked at him in surprise. 'Actual kidnappers, sir?'

'Yes. They're even trying to fish out who did it. They don't want their market to be destroyed. There's a lot you still have to learn about police work. We don't capture every criminal or solve every crime, so we partner with some of them. They let us know who is new in the business, who is doing what, who is planning what, that kind of thing.

'As long as they play according to the rules – no killing, no raping, et cetera – and they keep giving us good intel, we look the other way. They mostly snitch on their rivals.' He paused. 'This one has everyone scratching their heads. There has been no ransom call, no clues, nothing – only that live feed that the whole world watched. We're currently trying to figure out how the site was hacked; maybe that would give us something. JTF is already involved.'

'JTF?' I asked.

'Joint task force. Police, Army, Navy, Air Force, everyone. The police commissioner has taken over the investigation directly. He called me himself. Even Mr President has watched the video. People have recorded it. They've been sharing it on social media.' He sighed. 'I don't see how we will solve this one. I'm just praying that they somehow make a mistake.'

The same sense of unease as earlier came over me. The black hoodie. Maybe they'd already made a mistake. I bit my lip, but I couldn't stop myself.

'Sir, I think I saw something,' I said.

He turned to me expectantly. 'Well, let's have it.'

'It might be nothing, but there was a man – light-complexioned, slim, approximately my height. He came on a motorcycle. He hid his face behind a hooded top and dark glasses.'

'Go on.'

'He was looking at the house. I mean, the flat. He knew it was the top-floor flat.'

'Go on.'

'I was keeping an eye on him. I'm not sure, but something about him just put me on edge.'

'Is he still outside? How long ago was this?'

'He left when you arrived. Like I said, something just felt out of place, sir.'

'Instinct,' Balogun said, and smiled.

He raised his radio and gave instructions: 'Fatai, deploy two to Sule's van, urgent. POI exited estate on foot, minutes ago. ASP Fatokun leads. Await further details. Locate suspect.'

He slapped me hard on the shoulder.

'Good job! What are you waiting for? Go and get him.'

Chapter 6

As I hurried away from the building, my mind was racing. 'Suspect' sounded like a strong word to use. What if I was wrong? Also, the man had come on a motorbike; he could have left on another. The way those things weaved through traffic, there would be no chance of finding him.

It started to feel real when I got to Sule's van and a fully kitted-out officer handed me a bulletproof vest. People watched as the two officers assisted me with the Velcro straps. More news media had arrived. Reporters were speaking to cameras against the backdrop of the building. I saw a woman tapping her camerawoman and pointing to me. The camera swung towards us.

We had hardly closed the doors when Sule revved twice and did a skid start. I shot back into my seat and hurriedly buckled the seatbelt.

'Oga, did you see the person?' one of the men asked. His badge read 'Adewale'.

'He's about six feet, slim and light-skinned. Black hooded top, tight blue jeans and black Nike Airforce Ones.'

'Airforce One?' Adewale asked.

'Black Nike ankle boots.'

I was searching through the recorded clips when Sule stopped abruptly at the estate gate.

'Ol' boy,' he shouted at the young gateman in his starched green uniform. 'One yellow man like that just passed through here. He wear black hood an' pencil jeans. You see am?'

'I saw him,' the gateman said excitedly. 'A motorcycle brought him. He would have nearly reached the main road now. That's where the riders wait for customers.'

Sule screeched off and my phone almost fell out of my hand. I found the man we were looking for in a ten-second clip. I took a screenshot.

'This is him,' I said, showing my phone to the other officers. Still speeding, Sule took his eyes off the road to look at the photo.

We veered round a corner, our bodies flung to the side, then came to a screeching halt again. Had Sule spotted the suspect?

Up ahead, a police superbike with its headlight on was racing towards us. Sule pulled over to the side. The bike and what seemed like an endless convoy of black SUVs with tinted windows sped past us, sirens blaring.

As soon as the last vehicle passed us – an open-back van filled with armed men – Sule roared off again.

'Who was that?' I asked.

'Na the governor,' Sule replied, keeping his eyes on the road.

At that point, I realised how big the situation was. It had an international reach; a global audience, not just Nigerians, would have watched the video. The kidnappers had chosen the most popular Nigerian blog site on purpose. They wanted everyone to see Adams – to hear their prisoner's confession.

They were bold. What gave them such confidence?

I had no time to think about it. The main road loomed ahead. Like Adams' estate, there was an open gate just before the main road, but there was no one in sight manning it. The unofficial motorcycle taxi rank was just to the side of the gate, off the road on the other side of an open gutter. Someone had placed a plank across the gutter for the motorcycles to cross. Sule stopped right opposite it, blocking them in.

The black hoodie was nowhere in sight. I had

no idea how we would find him or if he really was important in any way. The more I thought about it, the more I doubted myself. But Abike had asked me to pay attention to the crowd for a reason; even I knew that criminals always return to the scene of the crime. Well, according to Hollywood. But why risk it?

I let the two officers, Adewale and Ekanem, take the lead. We had a growing crowd of onlookers as they showed the riders the picture on my phone. I saw people recording us on their own mobiles. Police vans raced past us in both directions. The city was in panic.

The Okada motorcycle riders, young men in their teens, spoke amongst themselves in Hausa as they passed my phone around, and then they started pointing. One of them, the one who held my phone, returned it to Adewale, who held on to it.

'They follow that way, now-now,' the boy said, pointing.

'He dey go Surulere,' another rider added.

'You know the plate number?' Ekanem asked.

To my surprise, they reeled off the licence plate number of the motorcycle the man had chartered.

We hurried back into the van. Sule had kept the engine on. Ekanem relayed information over his radio. I noticed the Okada riders gathered around one of their number, who was making a call on his mobile.

Everything seemed suspicious to me.

I silently cradled my doubt as we sped along. I was becoming less and less sure that the young man had anything to do with the kidnapping. For one, it must have taken a lot of time and resources to plan. Whoever was involved must have hacked the website long before, waiting till the time was right. The room they were holding Adams in would also have taken some preparing. The lights, the cameras for the live broadcast, the IV tube to keep him alive – I'd concluded that was what the thin tube was, even though his hands were bound behind the chair and I couldn't see a needle.

They must have also planned when and where to abduct him. It had not been by chance. Just like the live broadcast, asking him to confess his sins, they'd chosen his promotion party for maximum effect. These were not random upstarts or ambitious criminals; whoever had pulled this off was professional, resourceful and dedicated to their cause. They wouldn't make a mistake so simple as turning up in front of his house. It wasn't even the crime scene, for that matter.

I wished I'd taken Abike's advice and kept my mouth shut.

'Na him be that!' Sule shouted.

A large group of motorcycles had surrounded a driver and his hooded passenger up ahead. The commotion seemed to be an argument amongst the riders. They had caused a traffic jam, and with no traffic wardens in sight, enraged commuters were honking and attempting to edge past. I noticed that most of the bikes didn't have passengers. Could it be that they were holding the man captive for the police?

They were.

As soon as we arrived, the riders grabbed the unsuspecting man and held him down until Adewale and Ekanem could handcuff him and push him into the backseat of the van.

'What did I do?' the man kept asking.

With his hood down and his sunglasses missing, I realised that his paleness was due to albinism. He was in his late teens. He looked scared. Gazing at him from the front seat, I experienced a sinking sensation in my stomach.

'Where we dey go?' Sule asked.

The pit grew. I just knew I'd messed up. We couldn't take him back to Adams' house.

'Let's get out of here,' I said.

The bikers, motorists and a gathering crowd were watching us.

The young man kept asking what his crime was as we drove. Adewale and Ekanem searched him. They confiscated two mobile phones, a wallet, a lighter and a set of keys.

'Please, let me call my father,' he kept pleading.

I heard the fear in his voice, and I saw it on his face when I looked at him through the mirror. He was crying silently. I felt terrible.

'Can you call Abike?' I asked.

Adewale called her and handed his phone to me.

'We have him,' I said. I glanced in the mirror again. The young man looked terrified. I lowered my voice. 'He's just a kid.'

'Put me on speaker,' she said.

I did as she asked.

'Ekanem, Adewale, book him into Cell One and stay with him. No phone calls, no contact. Do not interrogate him. Call me when you get there. Fatokun, get onto an Okada and get back here straight away.'

Chapter 7

After a nerve-wracking Okada ride back to Adams' house, the first thing I noticed was the increased security, starting from the main road gate. A crowd had formed, talking amongst themselves and watching the armed personnel. The officers, for their part, were interrogating and searching people before letting them through. They were not letting any vehicles in.

I wobbled a bit as I got off the motorcycle and paid the daredevil rider the fare. The speed and recklessness with which he'd woven through traffic had left me wondering why he had a helmet and I, his passenger, didn't. But that was the least of my concerns. Faced with the security presence at the gate, I suddenly remembered that I didn't have an ID, I didn't have my uniform and I hadn't thought to get Abike's or anyone else's number that I could call to get through.

'ASP Fatokun?' a policeman said.

I nodded enthusiastically, and then I realised I need not have worried – I still had the bulletproof vest on. I was drenched in sweat beneath its weight.

Although Abike had the foresight to send someone to fetch me, we still had to walk down to the block of flats. As I approached on foot, I saw the excitement from another viewpoint.

Onlookers clustered on one side of the road, with news crews stationed just ahead of them. Across the divide, by the interior gate to the property, armed officers stood with AK-47s slung across their chests, eyes scanning the crowd. The scene looked less like crowd control and more like a stand-off: the people versus the government. It was in the way the locals spoke in low tones, glaring at the officers with resentment, and in the way the officers looked back – with suspicion and quiet contempt. I realised what had unnerved me about the crowd outside the gate to the estate, and earlier with the throng of Okada riders – a riot was simmering just beneath the surface.

I shook the silly thought out of my head. Surely the increased security was simply down to the governor's presence? There was no danger here.

Inside the compound, Abike was waiting for

me. Soldiers, police officers and men in dark suits and dark glasses were dotted around, all watchful and eerily silent. Someone had brought a table into the paved front yard and positioned three chairs behind it. A news crew was setting up microphones and checking the camera facing them. I recognised the logo of the Nigerian Television Authority – the state media.

Abike took me aside as I spoke, so as not to be heard.

'What did you see?' she asked.

'Just someone looking at the house. He also looked at me.'

'And that made him suspicious?'

'I believed he was watching me, and he knew which one was Adams' flat.'

Her voice was sharp. 'There are reports of unrest brewing all over the country because of this. You can't be picking people up just because you don't like the way they looked at you. What else was suspicious about him?'

I didn't get a chance to reply before the main door opened and even more security personnel poured out, with the governor, Ireti and SP Balogun behind them.

Up close, the governor was a smaller man than I had imagined from seeing his grinning face on billboards around the city lauding his great achievements, among them making Lagos State safe.

He spoke reassuringly to Ireti as the three sat down for the cameras. Her tense face and complete silence suggested that she was under considerable pressure.

Once the state media had secured the best positions, a security detail invited the other news crews into the compound to set up their cameras and microphones.

I stood with Abike on the other side of the cameras to watch the show.

'Good people of Lagos State,' the governor began, reading from a laptop. 'By now, you are all aware of the evil act broadcast on the internet at exactly twelve noon today. I want to assure you that every government body has been mobilised to rescue the brave officer, Chief Superintendent of Police Olakunle Babatunde Adams, and to apprehend the criminal elements responsible.

'Actions already taken include the special sitting of the joint chiefs of staff, the formation of a special joint task force on the order of his Excellency, President Francis Emeka Julius, and collaboration with Interpol and other international agencies. Most importantly, we have arrested a suspect who is currently assisting with the investigation of this crime.

'I have also directed the immediate arrest of the owner of the Natasha Gist Blog, the most popular blog in the country, and a special phone number has been set up for any information that can assist with the investigation. I want to assure you, the good people of Lagos State and Nigeria, that we will thoroughly investigate and uncover all co-conspirators in this most wicked act.'

I couldn't help but whisper to Abike, 'The site was hacked. Why is the owner being arrested?'

She ignored me.

The governor went on, assuring the people behind the cameras and microphones that the criminals would be found and dealt with to the full extent of the law. He concluded with:

'I hereby ask you all to pray for the safe return of SP Adams. I will take your questions now.'

There hadn't been a single mention of the distressed family.

The first question came from a tall woman with a shiny, shaven head.

'What will happen at twelve noon tomorrow?'

Caught up in the excitement, I had not considered this question. It should have been obvious: the first broadcast had been at noon, so it was safe to assume there would be another at noon the next day. It was clear that Adams' abductors meant to keep him alive for as long as his confession took; that was the purpose of the IV line. They had succeeded in preparing the entire world for another instalment of their horror show at noon the next day, and every day after that until they achieved their objective.

Every time I thought I'd understood how big this was, it kept getting bigger. Abike had mentioned reports of unrest. The rapidly expanding crowd at the main gate, the crowd outside the block and the media attention – they were all signs that breaking point was coming.

As soon as he'd made the most of his camera opportunity, the governor left.

Balogun walked up to me standing alone in the compound, unsure of what to do.

'What a day you're having, Fatokun,' he said.

Calling me by my surname felt strange. I'd introduced myself to Abike as 'Bobby', but she too was sticking to 'Fatokun'. I wondered what her first name was.

'Sir, what will happen to the man we arrested?'

I dared to ask. I wasn't sharing an unsolicited opinion, after all.

'Ah, yes. Your suspect. Well, we will start by torturing him before we begin any interrogations. That way, he will know that we mean business.'

What?

Balogun looked me dead in the eyes; the horror I felt was reflected back to me by his blank face. Then he broke. He held my arm for support as he bent over laughing.

We drew glances. He wiped actual tears from his eyes as he recovered.

His face still puffy from his fit of laughter, and suppressing giggles, he explained:

'I asked them to book him into Cell One – that is code for do-not-book. I don't think he's a suspect. Let me rephrase that: at this point, everyone is a suspect, but not someone who just showed up here on an Okada. Adams' daughter has confirmed his identity. He is a friend who saw the video and came to check on her. He should be home by now.'

'You didn't really think of him as a suspect when you told me to arrest him, did you?'

I kept forgetting to talk with deference and to use 'sir', but Balogun didn't seem to notice.

'Abike thinks he caught you filming him, and that's why he left in a hurry. But he was useful, and now he has served his purpose. We needed a suspect. The gang behind this thing will be monitoring the news. Right now, they will be wondering who is talking to us. The pressure could lead to them making a mistake.'

'What about the blog owner, sir?'

'What about her?'

'Are you really going to arrest her?'

'She has already been detained. You know, sometimes we look stupid, like we have no clue what we're doing, but it's simply because of orders from above. She was actually rather happy to be arrested. It will be a great story to blog about, instead of the cut-and-paste she usually does. She could have been bailed before she even saw the inside of a cell, but she was so eager that she refused the offer to call her lawyer. The officer I dispatched to invite her to the station informed me that she had already prepared herself for detention. She had packed some toothpaste, a brush, soap and sanitary products. She is going to take full advantage of this for her blog.'

'Is she still under arrest?'

'She's in a cell. She begged them to put her in with other prisoners. I put her in Cell One. Gave her VIP treatment. I do not want her interviewing inmates and putting words into their mouths on my watch! Rocky should have finished interrogating her about the hacking of her website by now. I'll discharge her when we get back to the station.'

'I thought Cell One meant do not book.'

'No. *Book* into Cell One means do not book; *put* in Cell One means book them into Cell One. It is a one-man cell that has AC, a small fridge, its own toilet and a TV. We reserve it for our VIP clients.'

'Hey!'

We both spun around. Neither of us had seen Abike approaching. She looked angry.

'Everybody saw you laughing,' she said through clenched teeth.

Balogun stood up straighter and looked around. I felt scolded, even though it wasn't me she'd meant. I wondered what it was about their relationship that gave her such freedom.

She looked from one of us to the other, doing nothing to hide her annoyance. It felt like my mother was telling off my sister and me.

'Rocky found something,' she said. 'We have to get back to the station, right now.'

Chapter 8

The briefing room was cramped. Abike was standing at the back with several other officers while I sat next to people I didn't know. A ceiling fan directly beneath a fluorescent light only managed to spread warm air. The two windows, which were small, both had heavy curtains over them.

Everyone was talking to someone except for me. At this point, I just wanted to get back to my hotel, take a long shower and try to make sense of the day.

When I'd arrived in the morning, I'd thought that I would be passed from person to person like I was at Panti, but instead I'd been thrust right into the middle of a kidnapping that was confusing even seasoned officers. What had I got myself into?

A slender young officer entered the room, walked to the front and plugged his laptop into a cable to the side of a large whiteboard. The subtle elegance and fluidity of his movement reminded me of Rotimi, a friend from primary school that the other kids had teased, mimicking his walk and calling him a girl. Last I heard he'd come out, and was living in Kenya with his partner and six kids.

The lights went off, and I feared it was a power failure, but the fan kept spinning. I understood the reason for the curtains when an overhead projector began to beam a still image of CSP Adams' ordeal onto the whiteboard. A black square covered the senior officer's exposed genitals.

'Hi, everyone,' the young man at the front of the room said. 'I am ASP Idowu, but everyone calls me Rocky. You're all welcome to Bar Beach Police Station.'

So this was the chap I was going to be working with.

Rocky aimed a laser pointer at the screen. 'Can anybody tell me where this is?'

Silence.

'Anybody? Any thoughts?'

'Somewhere in Lagos,' somebody said.

'We hope,' Rocky replied. 'I meant, what is this space he's being held in? This drown-chamber.'

He traced the edges of the screen with the red dot of his laser pointer.

I bet he was pleased with himself when he came up with 'drown-chamber'.

'Kidnappers' den,' somebody shouted from the back.

I almost chuckled. I turned around and all I saw were serious faces.

'A photographer's dark room,' someone else said.

'A swimming pool,' another person suggested.

'I like that,' Rocky said.

He turned to the screen and traced the chamber's edges with his red dot as he spoke.

'Using Adobe Photoshop, I estimate the width to be approximately 2.44 metres and the height to be 2.59 metres. That's 8 feet and 8.5 feet, respectively. Given his position, and assuming he's in the centre of the space, I estimate the length to be about 6.1 metres – 20 feet. He's in a standard 20 by 8 shipping container.'

A murmur spread as Rocky surveyed the room. He looked pleased with himself. He pointed the red dot at Adams' leg.

'Given the water level before and after,' he said, pointing to an image of two screenshots side by side, 'the water rose by approximately a foot in that last round. As the subject is six feet tall and sitting, his head is about four feet from the ground. That means the water is now around two feet below his nose – maybe less. If they continue at this rate, he has no more than two, maybe three rounds left before the water covers his face. That's two or three more broadcasts – before he drowns.'

People gasped. Someone invoked the blood of Jesus. Rocky scanned his audience. From the way he stood and surveyed the room, I sensed he was waiting for questions. I noticed that he referred to Adams as 'the subject'. Balogun stood up from the front row and took the pointer from him.

'Thank you, Rocky, you may sit now.'

I sensed Rocky's disappointment at his dismissal. He sat in the chair vacated by Balogun and crossed his legs.

'There you have it, people,' Balogun said. 'We're looking for a twenty-foot container. It's likely either in an isolated location, or it's been soundproofed. Rocky thinks the former is more likely, unless the soundproofing is on the outside of the container.

'We are looking for a device on top of the container to make the water delivery fast. A water tanker pipe would be the obvious solution, but it would be too visible. I'm thinking of a container prefilled with water on top of the container holding Adams.

'The information has already been shared with the joint task force and a grid search is in progress. The Navy and Air Force are providing air support; teams have already been dispatched to Apapa and Tin Can, and all other ports in the nation, and we are also cooperating with all neighbouring countries through Interpol.

'In other words, you don't have to bother with any of that. As Oga Adams is one of our own, our task is to use what we know about him to provide insight into who might be responsible for this. All of you here know Oga Adams, or you used to work with him before you transferred out of this station.

'The current theory is that this has something to do with a case he worked on. Your job is to comb through everything. Every criminal he put away, every name in every case he worked on since he came to this station is a suspect. Other stations are doing the same.

'You will work in teams of two. Anytime a name comes up, you put it on this board, and you alert an SP.

'People, whoever did this is not working alone. Someone built that drown-chamber. Someone hacked the website. Someone kidnapped Adams from the Officers' Mess.

Someone transported him to the container. One person cannot have all the required skills. It must be a gang. Find one of them, and we will find the rest.

'Let's find these bastards.'

Balogun gestured for me to follow him as the rest of the officers divided up the case files. Shutting his office door, he plopped into his chair.

'Sit,' he said.

I sat.

His voice was tired as he spoke. 'You see how police work is? It's not easy. It's not a joke. I hope you can keep up.' He softened slightly as he looked at me. 'That boy you arrested – you did the right thing. Instinct is your best friend in this job, while doubt is your enemy. Doubt will kill you. If you feel in your body that something is wrong, you have to act immediately. It's better to be wrong ten times than to be right one time but not listen to your instinct. Instinct is your guardian angel. She will guide you well in this job.

'Fatokun, I have a station full of seasoned officers working on this case, but you . . . you've been dropped into the deep end. You have the unique advantage of being an outside observer.

'All the officers out there, they're following what their training has taught them. They are following protocol. Until now, there's been no ransom demand. And based on that video, there won't be one. This is totally new. There is no protocol for this. So, without thinking too much, tell me what your gut tells you.'

No doubt, all the best minds in law enforcement were currently working on the case, and then there was me, a seasoned overthinker. I couldn't believe he'd asked.

I took a moment. 'I think it's personal, sir,' I said. 'The abductors said "sin", not "sins", so something specific. Something he did. Also, there's more than one person involved. He probably can't see their faces.' I realised it as I spoke. 'They used a synthesiser; they must have been in another room.'

Balogun raised an eyebrow. 'Obviously. They wouldn't want to get wet too. Okay. All of that is analysing evidence. Now, what does your gut tell you?'

I had a long way to go in this job.

'I think it's someone he knows. They really want to hurt him. This is revenge.'

'Good. So, who?'

'Someone in one of the cases he worked on.'

'And that's why we're going through all of

his records. We have people in Kirikiri prison talking to criminals he put away there. What else? Come on, Fatokun. Give me something good. Where else should we be looking?'

'His personal life. He seems to have several mistresses.'

'We call them girlfriends here. We've detained the ones we know. Speak from your instinct.'

He'd asked me not to think, but so far, it felt like I was letting myself down. I had to think.

'What if it's not about him?' I said. Something was forming in my head.

'I'm listening.'

'The voice said, "Confess your sin, and you shall be free." If he knew what it was, he could have easily just confess. Maybe he didn't confess because he doesn't know what the sin is.'

'Or, he knows that the moment he confesses, he will be killed.'

'Or that,' I conceded. So much for taking time to think.

'Did you notice that he doesn't know he's being recorded?' Balogun asked.

It was obvious as soon as he said it. I'd missed it.

'They're making sure he sees as little as possible. Now, that might mean that the person or persons involved do not want him to see their faces,' he said. 'Why? Either because they really intend to release him after he has confessed the sin, or they don't want to risk him saying something that would give their identity away, even though he doesn't know that he's being recorded. What does that tell you?'

I felt his eyes on me as I tried to think.

'Sir, what if he's not confessing because it's not his own sin that they want him to confess?'

'Who else's sin would it be?'

'The police force. Your station.'

Balogun sat up.

'Go on,' he said.

And boy, did I go on.

'Like you said, sir, it appears to be a very sophisticated operation – the planning must have taken a lot of time and patience. It appears to be the work of hacktivists working with very trained and resourceful individuals, which suggests militant activism. There are many such groups on the dark web that are active in social or political causes, particularly against the police force or the government. I believe we are looking for someone with resources who has an axe to grind.'

'An axe to grind,' he repeated.

'Yes. Someone who feels deeply wronged – enough to want to disgrace the police force.'

'Or the government.'

'Yes, or even the government.'

'Someone with a serious grievance against the government.'

'Yes, sir.'

'Like someone whose father was charged for conspiracy in plotting a coup.'

My heart leapt. Alarm bells rang in my head.

'Someone whose father was executed for treason.'

I felt weak all over.

Balogun stared at me with cold eyes. 'Someone like you.'

Chapter 9

'Were you ever going to tell me that you're Sir Fatokun's son?'

I was in shock. I didn't understand what was happening. How on earth did Superintendent Balogun know about my father? I was a child when it happened. It had been so long ago. And besides, everyone was happy to see the end of the military dictator who had overthrown a popular president. Political prisoners regained their freedom and became heroes. But my father had been executed and his businesses stolen. He was dead, and I had assumed that his story had died with him. How wrong was I?

He continued, 'Right now, everyone is suspicious of everyone else, and you arrived just when we discovered Adams was kidnapped, putting you right in the middle of the investigation. Rocky decided to do some digging and he found out who you really are – a computer expert with immense resources at his disposal and a reason to want to hurt the government. You do see how that could be suspicious, don't you?'

I didn't know what to say.

'Why were you keeping it a secret?' he asked.

'I wasn't keeping anything a secret, sir. It didn't occur to me to bring up my murdered father. What would be the point? And it wasn't my choice to come here – I was sent from Panti. I did not inject myself into the investigation – you asked me to go with Abike.'

'I know, I know. I'm not stupid. But you could have mentioned that your father was the billionaire industrialist. You people are still very rich, am I wrong? This begs the question: what are you really doing here? I mean, why the Nigerian police?'

He was right – money was not a problem. Only he did not know my mother.

It had taken years of negotiations to retrieve some of my father's properties. We never got back the factory that had made him rich, but we still came away with a little fortune. My mother, however, wouldn't let us live like we were rich – no splurging, no expensive holidays, no sports cars. We lived like the people around us when we arrived in London – other immigrant families watching the purse strings while working flat-out to provide a good education for their children. In fact, I didn't learn that we were somewhat wealthy until I was twenty-one and I had to sign some documents.

When the chance came to work for the Nigerian police, I saw it as an opportunity to carry out my own secret investigation into what had happened to some of the properties listed in my father's will; a lot of them in choice areas in Lagos had been sold multiple times since they were initially confiscated. The new owners had bought them from various shell companies. We suspected they were the very same people who had conspired with the military regime to frame my father for treason.

My mother still reminds me of how hard she tried to make me study law. She still thinks it's the only way we can get justice. I don't. I had planned to investigate the shell companies once I had access to government records. I won't rest until the conniving murderers are behind bars, and I intend to put them there.

'I've always wanted to be a police officer,' I lied. 'I guess I was being patriotic when I decided to join the NPF instead of the Met.'

If Balogun caught the sarcasm, it didn't show on his face. He studied me for a few seconds, then he leaned back in his chair and clasped his fingers behind his head.

'Everyone's jittery right now,' he said. 'Until we sort this thing out, every officer, including myself, feels like a target. Maybe it's better if you go home. There's really not much for you to do around here today, anyway. Go home, get some rest, and when this is over and nerves are a bit calmer, we can clear things up properly.' He met my eye. 'I think that would be the safest thing for you right now.'

I just wanted to get back to my hotel, take a long shower to wash off the sweat and madness, and order a bowl of *iyan* and *egusi* soup to have in the garden overlooking Lagos Lagoon. There was a huge screen out there where they aired live football or music videos when a band wasn't playing. Since I'd been there, it was always filled with an eclectic mix of interesting people.

When I'd first arrived at the hotel from Murtala Muhammed Airport, after checking me in, the lady at the front desk informed me that:

'We want you to enjoy your stay with us at Ten Rooms. Similarly, we want other guests to also enjoy their stay with us. This is a safe space for all people. As our guest, we ask you to respect all guests, visitors and staff, irrespective of your religious or moral views. Here at Ten

Rooms, we recognise that sexuality is a spectrum, and we love all the colours of the rainbow.'

It was both surprising and refreshing to learn that there was such a space in Lagos, considering the horror stories I'd heard back in the UK. My mother had chosen the hotel on her friend's recommendation. I wondered if her friend was queer, and if she was, I wondered if my mother knew.

Swaddled in the complementary *Adire* housecoat, I laid down and switched on the TV. It was tuned to CNN. I searched for local stations. None of them were mentioning the events of the day. Maybe it was being suppressed to avoid panic. Abike would probably say there was protocol. Or it wasn't as big as I thought it was.

But it was big. I knew it was. And I'd been there, right in the middle of it when it all kicked off. What a day I'd had. I saw Balogun's disapproving face. Even when I'd believed he was beginning to accept me, it had turned out that he was merely interrogating me, and I hadn't even realised it at the time. I saw Abike's unimpressed eyes measuring me and finding me lacking. She reminded me of my mother when I was young. Perhaps that was why I felt small in her presence. They both had the same no-nonsense look about them, as if for them there were better things to do with the face than smiling. I have watched men shrink before my mother, their egos checked by her indifference and unwillingness to indulge them. She was also frugal with her words, saying exactly what she wanted to say with just the words it took – no sugar-coating, just straight to the point, egos be damned. When Abike had scolded her superior for not being guarded with his laughter, that was my mother, only in a police officer's uniform. And when Balogun had accepted the rebuke with an instant apology, that was my father. Abike had trained Balogun like my mother had trained my father. Or Balogun was just like me and just like my father, instinctively recognising the alpha in the room.

Then there was Rocky. We hadn't spoken so far. It felt odd that he would investigate me like he had. I tried to see things from his perspective, but I doubted I would have suspected me if I were in his shoes. Whoever had pulled off the abduction had to be someone familiar with Lagos, or at least working with people who were. This was my first time in the country in almost twenty years; I didn't know anyone. But then, Rocky probably hadn't known that at the time.

Maybe he saw me as a threat. If so, that was on him, not me. But he was bright, I had to give him that. We had all watched the video, but he was the first to notice that Adams was in a shipping container.

Finding nothing on TV that held my attention, I fetched my laptop and settled at the desk in my suite. I navigated to the blog. The first post after the live broadcast was 'Natasha's Blog Hacked'. I respected her hustle. Go get your money, sis.

Natasha's second and latest post was a full video of Adams' ordeal. She had recorded it with her phone. The clip captured her gasps, a lot of *Oh my Gods* and her many abandoned attempts to narrate the unfolding horror:

'I think he's being held in some sort of torture room . . . Oh my God. Is this really happening?'

I watched the entire video again. Natasha had captured her arm reaching out to close the lid of her laptop when the floodlights went out, giving us a glimpse of her desk. I moved the slider back to before the water started falling, then expanded the paused clip to inspect the container. I was transfixed by the horror on Adams' face up close.

The post had generated a lot of comments.

I could relate to one that stated: 'I came for the video but I stayed for the comments.'

The more I read, the more I wanted to read. People were divided. As expected, a lot of them expressed shock and even left prayers for the victim and his family, but others saw things differently. For every concerned post, there were at least two venting anger at the police force. Someone who dared to defend the police attracted a deluge of replies cursing them and wishing that what was happening to Adams should happen to them too.

People were sharing personal stories of ordeals they'd endured at the hands of the Nigerian police. Reading such comments made me self-conscious about the institution I had become a part of. The picture they painted was of a force riddled with corruption and violent abuse of power, and even in league with criminals. 'I HOPE HE DIES' had received over a hundred likes.

At some point, it felt unhealthy to keep reading all the hatred. I returned to studying the paused image on the screen. The top wasn't visible. How had Rocky estimated the height of the container? The entire visible space was black. I expanded the image. I couldn't detect the corrugated ridges of a container wall.

What if Rocky had got it wrong? What if Adams was being held in a water tank?

In our home in Lagos, before we had fled to England, we'd had a huge water tank on top of a metal tower. It was filled up with water provided by the city when the taps ran, and for the times when it didn't fill up, my father paid for a water tanker to fill it. I used to watch as the men climbed up the tower and held a large hose down as it filled our tank with water.

What if Adams was being held in one such water reservoir tower in full view, while every cop in town was running around looking for shipping containers? All because Rocky had told them to.

I could be on to something. I imagined sharing my discovery with Abike. I pictured it – her impassive stare as I made my case; the slow sinking in of what it meant; her face lighting up as she realised that I'd just cracked the investigation wide open. I fantasised about calling her and surprising her with the results of my amazing gut instincts, then became conscious of the smile on my face. Why was I so desperate to impress her? I did wish I had her number. I wished I'd had the courage to ask for it. But we hadn't exactly started off well, and even if we had, I doubted she'd want me calling her outside of work – as honourable as I felt my intentions were.

I fetched the notepad and pencil by the bed and tried to focus my thoughts.

A shipping container made sense because it was already a sealed structure, but a water tank made even more sense as it was designed to hold water. I went online; Google informed me that shipping containers were indeed watertight, to an extent. But what about the smooth black wall in the video?

I inspected the expanded image again. If the black walls were some sort of rubber membrane to keep the water in, I would expect to see hints of the corrugated metal underneath.

Though I wasn't certain that Adams was being held in a shipping container, I still tried to imagine how such a drown-chamber would work. Maybe I could nail down the water delivery system because, as Balogun had said, surely they wouldn't just have a water tanker with its hose inserted into the top of a twenty-foot container next to it. Figure out the water, find the container, I mused.

I drew a line and stopped. Staring at the paper, I became aware of my excitement while thinking about the device. Had the person who'd designed Adams' drown-chamber experienced the same excitement when they'd come up with the idea? What had been going through their minds as they'd conceived, sketched and built it?

What goes on in the mind of a killer? I shuddered, my head full of images of drown-chambers. Whatever it was, I felt dangerously close to finding out.

I tore the page off, crumpled it and tossed it in the bin.

Chapter 10

When I got downstairs, I could see through the rear sliding doors that the garden was full. People were mingling about, staring at the screen. Had I known there was a match on, I would have gone down earlier to claim a seat.

It was only as I got closer that I sensed that something was wrong. Nobody was talking. There was no sound coming from the outdoor speakers. I saw the horror on the faces of the people who turned to look as I slid the door open. A man stood with his hands clasped over his head – the universal symbol of shock. I stepped out into the clammy warmth of the night, and I saw what they were all looking at.

It was the page the hackers had put up: Adams in a ceremonial uniform. Someone had decided to play the video on the big screen. That explained it; they must be just finding out about it. Then, as I got closer, I saw '18:00 WAT' flashing in red at the bottom of the screen, and the digital clock beneath it was ticking down to 6pm. It was live. My mouth flew open. I instinctively double-checked my watch – two minutes to go.

I didn't realise I'd sworn out loud until distressed faces turned to look at me. Just as quickly, they turned back to the screen.

I found a place to stand where I wasn't blocking anyone's view.

The screen turned black. It had the same timestamp in the bottom-right corner as on the first broadcast. Seconds passed. Then the floodlights shone upon Adams again. His head was bowed. He was motionless. I checked the level of the water. It hadn't risen further.

Slowly, Adams began to raise his head. He squinted at the lights. He was trying to see past the brightness.

The same altered voice read from the same ominous script:

'The wages of sin is death. Confess your sin, and you shall be free.'

Adams' face contorted with pain or regret.

'Please, I beg you, in the name of God,' he said. He was weak.

The voice repeated:

'The wages of sin is death. Confess your sin, and you shall be free.'

'I don't know what you want me to confess,' Adams wept.

I braced for the deluge of water; at noon it had happened after the voice had asked a second time.

'I swear, I don't know what you want me to say,' Adams pleaded. 'Please, I beg you, let me go. Please, in the name of God, don't do this. Please, don't do this.'

The voice asked a third time:

'The wages of sin is death. Confess your sin, and you shall be free.'

Adams broke down crying. His shoulders quivered; his slumped head swayed from side to side. He looked up, as if staring straight out at us. He filled his lungs and screamed.

'Talk!' someone shouted at the screen.

Water gushed down. It was harder watching it a second time. I held my breath with him. I didn't mean to. The water kept falling. Adams kept struggling in the chair, trying to breathe under the flood. When the water stopped, it had risen to his waist. He was coughing and shivering, from cold or from fear, or both. He looked down at the water lapping around his waist. He knew what was to come. Rocky's calculations were correct. Just like in a computer game, Adams only had two lives left. But this wasn't a game. If he didn't confess, his life would end.

The lights went off. Adams' coughing and gasping over the speakers was chilling. We were all glued to the screen, listening to him while the timestamp ticked the seconds away. He went silent. We were all silent with him. Thirty seconds went by. Then the screen abruptly changed to show the NTA News logo.

They'd hacked the national TV station! And they'd done it while everyone was waiting for noon tomorrow!

The screen transitioned again to the confused anchors on the national station's 6pm news.

The male anchor listened to instructions in his earpiece as he fiddled with the sheets of paper in front of him. 'It looks like we are back,' he said into the camera.

The entire garden broke out into excited discussions. No one was watching the screen anymore.

My heart was pounding. Whatever this was, it was way bigger than I'd thought. Hacking a blog site was one thing; hacking into the live broadcast of the national TV station was another. I imagined what was going on at Bar Beach Police Station. No doubt they would all still be there, working through the night until they cracked the case. They would also likely have watched the last broadcast live, although, like me, they'd all expected the next horror show to be at noon the next day.

I felt I should be there, helping in some way, but Balogun had made it clear that I wasn't welcome, at least not for the time being.

All around me, people were talking about Adams' situation. I was witnessing the same split of sentiments as I'd read in the comments online.

A debate soon established itself between the two camps. One side shouted their support for the abductors, while the other side tried to shout them down. I wondered which side I would be on if I hadn't enrolled in the police force.

'We're not at war with each other,' a chubby woman said, her commanding voice rising above the chaos. 'We can disagree and still be civil.'

Someone shouted back, 'Thunder fire you and civil,' – a Nigerian curse I hadn't heard since I was a boy. There was laughter – as if we hadn't just watched a man being tortured live on TV.

'We don't want issues with our neighbours,' the woman said sharply. 'Let's keep it down if we can't keep it civil.'

No one listened to her.

The debate continued in the same manner – a competition of vocal cords as one side shouted their arguments and the other side countered. Those on the side of the police were losing.

'Personally, I don't care about the police,' a man yelled. 'But what these people are doing is uncalled for. That man probably has a family. Imagine how they're feeling watching him like that.'

'What about all the innocent people killed at the hands of the police?' a woman shot back. 'These days, encountering a police checkpoint in the middle of the night is just as dangerous as running into robbers.'

'Me, I don't care about the man or his family,' another man said. 'My own worry is that they are giving Nigeria a bad name.'

Someone raised both their arms and kept them up. I hadn't noticed them before then. It was Hyacinth. I'd met them on the night I checked in. I'd gone out to see the garden, and they were there smoking a hookah pipe with a group sitting on a mat right by the water. They'd invited me over and had been somewhat disappointed that I didn't smoke. I'd stayed with their party anyway, and we'd discussed politics and Nollywood. Hyacinth was non-binary. All their friends were queer too. They either worked for or owned a brand image consultancy. I tried to remember its name.

People fell silent one by one as they noticed Hyacinth's raised arms. Their colourful bangles gathered at their forearms.

When everyone was silent, Hyacinth spoke with the same calm, gentle voice and measured cadence from the night we'd met.

'My girls got engaged, so we threw them a party,' they said. 'We just wanted to celebrate their love. It was a small affair. Just friends. Queer folk and allies. Nothing big. It was at my old place. Someone must have tipped off the police.

'They busted the door. They came with four vans. You would think they were responding to a bank robbery. They took us all to the station. They gave us a choice: pay up or be charged under Section 4. They were asking for 100K per person. Whoever couldn't pay would be charged in court the next morning.

'I didn't have that kind of money. The couple didn't have *shi-shi* in their account – you know how the economy is. Luckily, I'd invited a client. A very monied somebody. She offered to pay for us all. They made her transfer the money that evening – 5.5 million naira. Had she not been there, we would all have been looking at fourteen years.'

Hyacinth pointed at the screen now showing the news.

'That was the bastard who led the raid,' they said.

Everyone remained silent.

'Oh, he can burn in hell then.' It was a man who had been sympathetic to Adams. He demonstrated washing his hands of the officer's fate.

'Let him drown,' someone else said.

I was staring at Hyacinth across the crowd, trying to catch their attention, when someone pointed at the screen and hushed everyone.

What now?

We all watched. A passing motor boat's engine filled the sudden silence. The news segment was still in disarray, with the anchors visibly listening for instructions through their earpieces.

'What is it?' someone asked.

'They will say it again,' a woman said.

We all waited. I scanned around. All eyes were on the screen, watching the fidgeting anchors. The man was rearranging his papers again. We watched and waited, just like we had when the floodlights on Adams had gone off and no one had dared take their eyes off the black screen shrouding his torment.

Wait. Something had just occurred to me. Out there in the garden overlooking the lagoon, we had all continued watching the live broadcast even after the screen went black. We had kept watching until the live feed ended and the hackers ended their seizure of the news channel.

My body prickled.

In her blog post, Natasha had stopped recording when the floodlights had gone off.

I'd watched the first broadcast live, and just like this time, when the lights had gone off, we'd all been glued to the screen, waiting to see what happened next. Natasha, however, had closed her laptop and turned her camera to herself when the lights had gone off. It was as if she knew there wasn't anything more to come.

My heart leapt. I looked around for someone to share the discovery with, but my excitement was cut short when the onscreen anchors started talking at the same time. The male anchor paused and turned to the female anchor.

'We are being informed that, by executive order, His Excellency the President has declared any viewing of the live or recorded video of CSP Adams in captivity to be illegal.'

The garden erupted in jeers, shouts and laughter.

I didn't have time to dwell on the stupidity of the government. Following on from my hunch about Natasha, something had also occurred to me about Rocky. What if my instincts about him were right?

He was probably aware of Adams' extortion racket. He referred to Adams only as 'the subject'.

If he was gay, like my friend Rotimi, then he had a motive.

What if Rocky had led everyone on a wild goose chase with his container theory? An insider had to have been involved in kidnapping a senior police officer from a party at the Police Officers' Mess – someone Adams knew and trusted.

The sudden realisation caused my mouth to fall open in shock.

I had to warn Balogun. But I didn't have his number. I didn't have Abike's number. I didn't have anyone's number. And there was no such number as 999 to call either – I had been shocked to learn that this was still the case after so many years. To make matters worse, I had also been told to stay away from the station. But what if Rocky belonged to the group that carried out the kidnapping? He could have been pulling our strings from the inside all along, and I had to tell someone.

Chapter 11

Someone tapped my shoulder. I jolted and spun round. It was Hyacinth. The chubby lady was with them. I did my best to compose myself. I could be polite for a minute before making my excuses and figuring out what to do.

'Bro,' Hyacinth said, 'how are you?'

'Not bad.'

'I mean, after watching that.'

I shrugged. They turned to their companion.

'This is Bobby. He came from Jand to become a Naija policeman.'

'Really? Why?'

I shrugged. I was starting to expect the bewilderment when people learned that I'd relocated to Nigeria to join the police.

The lady ignored my extended hand and claimed a hug instead.

'You're room 7,' she said. 'I'm Jasmine, the proprietor of this magical space.'

'So, which one do you think it is?' Hyacinth asked me.

I was lost. They read it on my face.

'You know – Romans 6:23. "The wages of sin is death." Which sin do you think it is? Jasmine and I have been debating, and so far, we've already eliminated the obvious ones. You know, the first five: no other gods, no graven images, no taking his name in vain, no working on the sabbath.'

They counted them off their fingers. They got stuck on the fifth.

Jasmine helped them: 'Respect your parents.'

I wondered if they were a couple. As if to answer my thought, they both locked fingers.

'Yes, that one,' Hyacinth said. 'Honour your mother and father, no matter how much trauma they've caused you. That one.'

'My money is on don't murder and don't steal,' Jasmine said.

'But I think it's thou shalt not do your neighbour's wife,' Hyacinth retorted. 'No one's as motivated as a spouse who's been cheated on. What about you, what do you think?'

I was distracted, thinking of what Biblical clues we might have overlooked. I considered every permutation of 6–2–3 to see if the timing of the broadcasts had been hidden in there all along.

'It must have been really hard for you to watch,' Jasmine said gently.

I nodded. 'It was harrowing.' I didn't know the man; the evidence was that he was a piece of shit, but he was a human being, undergoing torture live on air against the rising threat of drowning. And I suspected I knew who was responsible – at least two of them. I had to get to the station. I had to tell Balogun.

But what if I was wrong? My initial certainty that it was Rocky had begun to waver, and suddenly I wasn't so sure.

But what if I was right?

'You look like a man who has to be somewhere,' Hyacinth said.

'I do. But I don't have a car.'

'We have a car and a driver,' Jasmine said. 'He can take you anywhere.'

I hesitated to accept the offer.

'Go and do what you have to do, Judas,' Hyacinth said, and that settled it for me.

It was already dark, but the heat was terrific. I had started sweating in the garden. I looked forward to the air-con during the ride.

The car was a black Prado with Ten Rooms' logo on its sides and the driver an elderly man with three vertical tribal marks on both cheeks. He reminded me of my late father's friend, Engineer Awe, an Egba man.

'Where are we going, sir?' the gentleman enquired as I fastened my seatbelt in the passenger seat next to him.

'*Ekaale.*' I greeted him with a slight bow. I refused to get used to old people addressing me as 'sir'. I shook hands with him. 'My name is Bobby. Please, can you take me to Bar Beach Police Station?'

'Hope no problem, sir?' he said.

'No, sir,' I replied.

'*Alhamdulilah*,' he said. 'Moshood is my name.'

We shook hands and I thanked him. '*Ese*, sir.'

Sadly, the air-con wasn't working, and when I asked Moshood to please wind down the rear windows, he smiled and said, 'It is not safe.'

It was late, but the traffic had not relented. Car exhaust and other unknown smells filled the cabin. I watched motorcycles weave through the smallest gaps. I wondered if I should have taken one; at least I wouldn't be sweating so much with the wind rushing over me. Now I had no choice but to sit and wait in the sweltering conditions of the Prado, contemplating what I would say to Balogun.

We were on Ahmadu Bello Way, approaching the turning to the station, when I saw Rocky standing at the junction with his phone pressed to his ear.

'Stop here,' I said.

Moshood slowed and pulled up at the side of the road.

'Stopping here is not allowed,' he said, checking his mirrors.

'Don't worry,' I said. 'I'm a police officer.'

I felt him watching me, but I was watching Rocky. My phone vibrated in my pocket. I didn't take my eyes off him as I grabbed it. Taking a quick glance at the screen, I saw that the call was from my mother, who must have heard about the kidnapping. I imagined how the conversation would go. I let it ring out, but it started up again. As I debated whether or not to answer, Moshood cautioned me.

'Area boys snatch phones here,' he said. He looked in his mirrors as if he were searching for potential threats.

She kept trying to reach me. I knew she wouldn't stop until she had spoken to me and tried to convince me to rethink my mad decision to join the police here, but it wasn't the time. I sent a message: 'At work. Can't speak. Talk later.'

I looked up. Rocky was surveying the area as if he was searching for someone. A black SUV pulled up ahead of him. With his phone to his ear, he watched the SUV, then put the phone in his pocket and checked behind him. He walked up to the car and the back door opened. It was too far away to read the registration number. He cast a last glance behind him before climbing in. He had barely shut the door when the SUV moved off.

What little doubt I may have had was gone. Rocky was acting in a shady way because he was up to something shady.

Balogun had told me to listen to my instincts. 'Follow that car,' I said.

Moshood looked at me. 'You sure say you be policeman?' he asked.

'Yes.' I hoped he didn't ask for my ID. 'Don't let them know you are following them. I want to see where he's going.'

He studied me for a moment, then shrugged and checked his mirror before pulling out onto the road.

I didn't have a plan; I hadn't had one when I'd asked to be driven to the station, and I hadn't had one when I'd spotted Rocky looking dodgy and decided to tail him. I just knew that I had to know where he was going.

My phone vibrated with a new message. 'Call

me ASAP,' my mother had texted. I returned the mobile to my pocket.

We pursued the black SUV across Lagos Island and onto the mainland. I increasingly suspected that Rocky was attempting to flee.

The thing about Lagos is that it is both a city and a state. And the state is large – 1,292 square miles, to be precise. About twenty million people live there, so it's a good place to hide if you know your way around.

'I think they're going to Ilashe,' Moshood said.

The SUV was a good distance ahead. The traffic had thinned, and we were the only two cars on the highway.

'What's there?' I asked.

'The beach. There are plenty of hotels.'

'You are familiar with the place?'

'Yes. I used to carry some of our guests to go to the beach house there.'

With the SUV a good distance ahead, Moshood slowed down and turned onto a side road.

'What are you doing?' I asked, alarmed.

'If I continue, they will know we are following them.'

We had been travelling for almost three hours. We were well out of town now.

'But we'll lose them,' I said.

'I know where they're going. This is the only way in and out. I will just give them ten minutes, then we will continue.'

'Where are they going?'

'Container Village.'

I almost screamed.

'Container? Like, shipping containers?'

'Yes. They use shipping containers to build rooms and parlours. Foreign students like to lodge there. It is not as expensive as other places.'

Containers converted into rooms for rent, a long way out of town. Rocky had some explaining to do, but not to me. If he wasn't planning to hide in the Container Village, he had to be meeting with his co-conspirators. There was only one way to find out.

'Let's go,' I said.

We drove down a sandy road through a small village of beach houses. Ahead, where the Atlantic met the moonless sky, everything dissolved into inky blackness. We turned left onto an even sandier track, and the headlights caught a row of black-painted containers amidst tall palm trees. Their broad sides faced the sea. At the end of the row stood a black SUV, parked behind the last of the converted units. There were only four in total, though I'd expected more. We were the only other car.

Moshood turned at the end of the road. Driving back past the parked-up SUV, I got a better look inside. It appeared to be empty. We drove back the way we'd come and pulled up behind the first of the container huts. He switched off the lights and killed the engine, plunging the road into darkness. The sound of the sea replaced the hum of the tyres on the sand.

'This is the first phase,' he said. 'On another site, they have more containers, but they haven't started converting them. They say they will have a swimming pool there.'

Empty containers on a construction site on a beach in the middle of nowhere.

The black SUV started up, beginning a two-point turn as we had done. It had been empty when we had driven close to it. I'd missed the driver coming out.

'Should I follow them?' Moshood asked.

I shook my head, slinking down in my seat as they approached. After the headlights swept past, I looked up and saw the car turn back onto the exit road we'd come down.

'Did you see who was in the car?' I asked.

'The light entered my eyes,' he said, 'but I think it was two people.'

I thought so too. They had come to check

on something in the container – or someone. None of the containers had a water tanker parked nearby, so Adams couldn't be held in any of them. Why had they come all that way, only to leave after spending so little time there?

I steeled myself. 'If I'm not back in ten minutes, call your boss and tell her where we are. Tell her to go to Bar Beach Police Station and ask for SP Balogun. Describe the car that we followed. Tell her it picked up Rocky close to the station and brought him here. Also, tell her about the second phase of the container village.'

I opened the door and the cabin light came on. Moshood, fully clued in to the secret nature of our adventure, quickly switched it off.

'Is it about that policeman they kidnapped?' he asked.

I nodded. I felt like a hero as I stepped onto loose sand, amidst the sound of the sea and the palms whistling in the wind.

My heart pounded as I walked up to the back of the container and placed my head against it. I didn't hear any sounds from inside. I crept along the side and stopped. There was light emanating from the front of the structure. The sea lapped at the shore, about twenty metres away. I peeped round the corner. A wooden deck appeared to run the length of the container.

The light was from inside, beaming through glass sliding doors.

My heart raced. I'd assumed the hut would be empty. If the lights were on, someone could be inside. Perhaps the person Rocky had come to meet. One thing was clear – it wasn't where Adams was being held.

I considered returning to the car to make the call myself. As I was still negotiating with my brain, my feet took charge. I stepped forward and saw the back of a person standing on the edge of the deck. My heart leapt and I quickly retreated. Thanks to the whispering palms, they'd not heard me. A moment later I smelled cigarette smoke blown back by the breeze.

Adrenaline was coursing through my system, making me bold beyond my ability. I slowly edged forward again.

It was Rocky. He was facing the sea, puffing smoke into the breeze.

Just do it, my brain said.

I walked out of my hiding place. I was happy with the way I startled him.

'What are you doing here?' he asked, backing away as I climbed the steps onto the deck. His shock made me bolder. He couldn't see how hard my heart was beating under my sweat-soaked shirt.

'I could ask you the same,' I said.

Rocky looked scared. He dropped his cigarette on the deck and stamped it out, looking around frantically.

'Come inside,' he said. He stepped inside the container, but I remained where I stood.

'Now,' he insisted. 'Before they see you.'

'Who?' I asked. I didn't budge.

He spoke frantically. 'An informant. If they see you, they will think it's a set-up.'

'Who is the informant?' I asked.

'I don't know. This is the first time I'm meeting them. Come inside.' He looked genuinely scared.

'Did they tell you Adams is being held in a container?' I asked.

He nodded. 'Yes, yes. Come in.'

I walked towards him. He reached out, grabbed my wrist and yanked me inside. He was stronger than he looked. He did another quick scan then slid the door shut. Next, he hurriedly pulled the blackout curtain over the length of the glass frontage, then turned to face me.

'Fatokun, what the hell are you doing here?' he asked.

He had recovered from the shock of my arrival, and now he looked pissed off.

'It's a free country,' I said.

'Are you staying here?'

I noticed his eyes narrow with suspicion. He'd said he was meeting his informant for the first time. He had every reason to be even more suspicious of me.

'Did you find the informant or did they find you?' I asked.

Something felt wrong. I couldn't put my finger on it, but my instinct, if that was what it was, kept telling me that something wasn't quite right.

'Fatokun, you haven't told me what you're doing here.'

'I followed you from the station. You got into an SUV. It looked rather suspicious. I wanted to know where you were going.'

'You followed me? How? Why?'

'Because you might have sent the entire police force on a wild goose chase. I suspected you were involved – now I know I'm right. Have you considered that your informant might have lied to you? Maybe Adams is not being held in a container.'

'Fatokun, I am a *real* police officer. This is not a game. If you had suspicions, you should have gone to Balogun.'

'Like you did,' I said. I hated the way he

stressed the word 'real'. 'Did you tell Balogun about your informant?'

He fixed me with a deathly stare.

'I thought as much,' I said. 'Let me guess, this informant told you not to tell anyone, correct?'

He just stared at me. Something was forming in my head. It was all making sense.

'They told you that you can't trust anyone, didn't they? And now they've lured you out here to a place where nobody would know you'd come to meet someone.'

'Fatokun, you're going to ruin everything.'

'Call Balogun now,' I said. 'Tell him what you know.'

Rocky put his finger to his lips. Someone had climbed onto the deck outside. He looked around and pointed at a door next to the kitchenette on the right side of the space. I understood. I assumed it was the bathroom. I tiptoed and carefully opened the door. Just as carefully, I shut it behind me. I stood perfectly still in the darkness and listened.

Then I heard a sound behind me.

Chapter 12

I came to in total darkness, a terrific headache throbbing where I'd been clubbed on the head. I immediately knew I was tied to a chair in a container. I struggled to free myself. I screamed like a trapped animal, knowing it was futile.

This was the way I would die.

My mother had been against me going to Nigeria. She said the country killed people for fun. My sister, Mimi, had been excited. She'd confided in me that she'd been to Nigeria for a party in Lagos. Twice.

My father had objected too, even though he'd been dead since I was a boy. He was still alive in my dreams – telling me off, setting me straight or just being there, like a permanent part of me. He'd shaken his head, just like he'd done when I was a boy. He hadn't liked the idea one bit, but he also hadn't brought up the police's hand in his false conviction. My dreams hadn't caught up to his passing, but neither had his ghost, which kept on living in them.

I would never see him again. I would never see any of them again – not Mimi, not my mother. Perhaps I would live on in their dreams, and they too wouldn't be able to dream of me dead.

They were flashbacks. I was lucid and I was calm. Too calm. I had accepted my fate.

I wasn't ready for flashbacks. Not yet. I wasn't ready to die. Not like this. Not for other people's sins.

I filled my lungs and screamed so hard I couldn't hear my own voice. I'd tear my hands from my wrists if I had to. Drowning was the worst way to die.

I screamed like I'd never screamed before.

But nobody heard me.

Then I began to cry alone in the dark.

How fickle is life? How easily it ends. One stupid mistake, one wrong turn, one bad decision is all it takes. If only I had never learned about that recruitment event in London. If only I had never replied to the email. If only I had listened to my mother. If only Nigeria hadn't killed my father.

A light came on. I flinched.

It wasn't the bright light of floodlights; it was the glow of a laptop screen on a chair in front of me. I recognised the Nigerian Police Force homepage.

I already knew I wasn't naked. I looked up; there was no hole above my head, no IV line in my arm and nothing lining the corrugated walls of the container.

Moshood. Had he called his boss like I'd asked? Had he relayed my message? Was he in a container like me? Had they snuck up on him in the car?

I remembered hearing someone behind me in the bathroom. I remembered the blow just as I was turning. I'd seen stars.

Rocky. Where was he? What had happened to him? Had he sent me into the bathroom knowing someone was in there?

Was he also trapped in a container?

I'd known something was wrong. I'd sensed it. Rocky had been lured into a trap. Maybe that's how they'd got Adams as well. Maybe the senior officer had also crept away to meet with an informant. Maybe someone with a vendetta against the Nigerian police was abducting officers and I had offered myself up to them for free. I groaned with regret.

The screen flickered. Adams' picture stared at me. The counter beneath his face was counting down to midnight. Fifteen minutes to go. This time they had hacked the Nigerian Police Force website.

Why were they keeping me alive? Why were they making me watch?

I searched for speakers in the darkness. Was anyone going to talk to me? Did they know I was new to the job? I didn't even have a uniform yet.

Time became strange. I didn't know how long I'd been there and I didn't know how long it had been since I'd woken up. But fifteen minutes seemed to go past in a flash.

It was as if facing imminent death had brought the precious nature of time into sharp focus. It was running out – for Adams, and for me.

The screen turned black. I heard Adams' voice. He sounded weak. He was singing in the dark, mumbling the words to 'Amazing Grace'.

On the screen, the floodlights came on. He raised his head towards the beams and continued singing, turning his face to the side to avoid the blinding glare.

I waited for the words.

'The wages of sin is death. Confess your sin, and you shall be free.'

Adams seemed to roll his eyes at the camera. He continued singing.

'The wages of sin is death. Confess your sin, and you shall be free.'

I willed him to tell them what they wanted to hear. I didn't want to watch him drown. Would they do that? Would they kill a person on a live broadcast?

Adams suddenly looked straight ahead and screamed long and loud, his eyes shut, his mouth opened wide.

Water crashed down upon him. I held my breath. He kept on screaming until he choked, but even then he struggled to recover and managed to scream in between panting gasps.

When the water stopped, it had risen to his chest. The surface shimmered under the brilliance of the floodlights.

Rocky's calculations were spot on. Nonetheless, Adams had one chance left.

He shook his head like a dog shaking water from its fur, then he filled his lungs and screamed again. It resonated in my body.

He wasn't screaming for help; he was done playing by their rules. He screamed himself hoarse. He screamed himself to exhaustion. He panted as he stared straight into the camera. His face was wild and resolute. He was prepared to die. I wasn't prepared to watch it happen.

'The wages of sin is death. Confess your sin, and you shall be free.'

I braced to watch a man drown on camera.

Adams' shoulders quavered as he broke into laughter.

I waited for the water. I wasn't sure I would be able to watch. Seconds ticked by. It was taking longer than before. Then the voice spoke again.

'The wages of sin is death. Confess your sin, and you shall be free.'

Adams had called their bluff! They weren't going to do it. They weren't going to drown a man on a live broadcast. I felt a tiny drop of hope.

'To hell with you,' Adams growled. He was weak, but he wasn't broken. I admired his defiance.

I felt as if I was with him in that drown-chamber, the water rising up my body too. His fate and mine were tied in that moment. After him, it would be my turn. I'd been rooting for a miracle – for him, for me. Maybe we already had one.

The voice spoke again.

'The wages of sin is death. Confess your sin, and you shall be free.'

My heart had never beat so fast while sitting. I waited, hoping that the water didn't fall again – hoping that they never planned to cross that line.

Adams burst into laughter again. He laughed as if he was truly amused. Was he losing it? Had he lost it?

I feared that he would provoke them to let the water fall again, but the voice spoke.

'The wages of sin is death. Confess your sin, and you shall be free.'

Adams kissed his teeth.

'The wages of sin is death. Confess your sin, and you shall be free.'

He watched in silence.

With each recital of the question without the water falling, my glimmer of hope grew. Then the voice went off script:

'You have one chance left. Do you want a clue?'

Chapter 13

'Take the clue. Come on, take the goddamn clue!' I shouted at the screen.

Adams' nod was so slight, I almost didn't see it. And after I did, I wondered if I really had.

'Cell One,' the voice said.

Adams looked confused.

'December 16th,' the voice added.

Adams' eyes bulged. He knew his sin.

'The wages of sin is death. Confess your sin, and you shall be free.'

'It was the work of the devil,' Adams stuttered.

I saw the tears fall from his eyes.

'I'm sorry,' he said. 'I'm sorry. I'm sorry.'

'The wages of sin is death. Confess your sin, and you shall be free.'

'Oh God, I'm sorry. It wasn't meant to happen like that. I'm sorry. Oh God, please, I'm sorry.'

'The wages of sin is death. Confess your sin, and you shall be free.'

'Please forgive me!' Adams screamed. 'I'm sorry! I'm sorry!'

'Confess, and you will be free.'

'Oh God. Who are you people?'

'Are you ready to confess your sin?'

'Please forgive me. Please.'

'The wages of sin is death. Confess your sin, and you shall be free. Confess, now.'

I watched Adams staring into his memory. His face crumpled as he remembered. He shook his head in regret.

'Now,' the voice said.

Adams began.

'We arrested some boys.'

'Boys or men?'

'Young men.'

'Where?'

'At a party.'

'What kind of party?'

'It was a gay party.'

'The men were gay?'

'Yes.'

'How did you know about the party?'

'An informant told me.'

'Who was it?'

'A police officer.'

'What is his name?'

'We call him Rocky.'

'Fuck!' I cursed out loud.

'Is Rocky gay?' the voice asked.

'Yes.'

'What happened to the men?'

'We asked them to give us money, or else I would charge them.'

'How much did you ask for?'

Adams hesitated.

'How much?'

'One million each.'

'Bastard!' I screamed at him. I remembered Hyacinth's story. Were they watching this too?

'Why?' the voice asked.

'Because they were rich.'

'All of them?'

Adams shook his head. 'No. Just one of them.'

'How did you know this?'

'Rocky told us.'

'The rich one – who was he?' The questioner was relentless.

'Please, don't do this,' Adams begged.

'Who was he?'

'The son of retired Major General Dele Akindele.'

'Did he pay the money?'

'No. He said that his family knew about his sexuality. He said we should call his father.'

'Did you call his father?'

'No.' Adams sounded on the verge of tears again.

'What did you do?'

'I detained him.'

'In Cell One.'

'Yes, sir.'

The voice was impassive. 'Is that where you killed him?'

What? I stared at the screen in disbelief.

'No, sir. Please, forgive me. It was the work of the devil.'

'Is that where you killed him?'

Adams broke down in tears.

'You must confess your sin,' the voice said.

'Sir, please, it was all a mistake.'

'Confess. Now.'

'When I returned to the station in the morning, he told me what happened to him in the night.'

'What happened to him?'

'Some officers touched him.'

'Touched him?'

'They slept with him.'

'Slept with him?'

Adams' voice broke. 'He said they raped him.'

'Were these officers male?'

'Yes.'

'What are their names?'

'Santana and Meji.'

'After the man you detained in your VIP cell was raped by two male officers, what did you do?'

Adams cried like a baby.

'Did you order his execution?'

The question echoed in the room, and I watched as Adams nodded in reply.

I groaned. There were no words.

'To cover up what happened?' the voice asked.

Adams nodded. 'It wasn't my choice. They all agreed that we couldn't let him go. It was out of my hands. If I didn't cooperate, they would have killed me too. Please have mercy on me. It was never supposed to happen like that.'

'The wages of sin is death.'

'Please forgive me!' Adams screamed. 'Please forgive me! I'm sorry! I'm sorry!'

He kept begging, his voice raw, but the voice remained silent.

Adams began to cry once more, shaking his head as he wailed. Tears streamed down his face. He sobbed uncontrollably.

Still, the voice said nothing.

I couldn't believe what I'd just heard. The whole world had heard it too. The bastard deserved to die. But that wasn't the abductors' plan. They didn't want vengeance. They wanted exposure. Justice.

I imagined the rest of Adams' gang of corrupt officers being arrested right now, or running. I hoped every last one of them was caught. Surely they would face a firing squad. I didn't believe in that, but for these monsters, I was willing to make an exception. The fucking bastards.

Adams kept crying.

Then, suddenly, his head jerked up. His eyes bulged toward the ceiling.

The water came crashing down.

Adams shook violently. The water kept falling. He was fighting for his life. As the water rose to his chin, he tilted his face up into the downpour. It kept rising, splashing over his face, creeping up his cheeks. Soon, his head was submerged. The torrent stopped. Adams jerked violently under the water. A ream of bubbles streamed up. Then he stopped moving. A single, final bubble broke the surface. The water glittered as its ripples spread.

This wasn't justice; this was murder. I wished that the water would fall away in one sudden gush. I willed Adams to escape his constraints and burst through the surface. But the water had settled. It was over.

The lights stayed on. The timestamp continued ticking by. The screen split into nine squares: Adams' submerged chamber was at the top-right corner, surrounded by eight other chambers with eight empty chairs.

Alone in the dark, all that was left to do was wait.

Bobby Fatokun will return in
Fall From Grace.

September 2026.

About Quick Reads

"Reading is such an important building block for success"
— Jojo Moyes

Quick Reads are short books written by bestselling authors.

Did you enjoy this Quick Read?

Tell us what you thought by filling in our short survey. Scan the QR code to go directly to the survey or visit:
bit.ly/QuickReads2026

Thank you to Penguin Random House, Hachette and all our publishing partners for their ongoing support.

A big thank you to Curtis Brown for supporting the 20th anniversary of Quick Reads.

A special thank you to Jojo Moyes for her generous donation in 2020–2022 which helped to build the future of Quick Reads.

Quick Reads is delivered by The Reading Agency, a UK charity that inspires social and personal change through the proven power of reading.

readingagency.org.uk   @readingagency   #QuickReads

The Reading Agency, Registered number: 3904882 (England & Wales)
Registered charity number: 1085443 (England & Wales)
Registered Office: 24 Bedford Row, London, WC1R 4EH
The Reading Agency is supported using public funding by Arts Council England.

Find your next Quick Read

For 2026 we have 6 Quick Reads for you to enjoy:

Quick Reads are available to buy in paperback or ebook and to borrow from your local library. For a complete list of titles and more information on the authors and their books visit: **readingagency.org.uk/quickreads**

Continue your reading journey with The Reading Agency:

Reading Ahead

Challenge yourself to complete six reads by taking part in **Reading Ahead** at your local library, college or workplace: **readingahead.org.uk**

Book Club Hub

Join the **Book Club Hub** to find a book club and discover new recommendations: **bookclubhub.co.uk**

World Book Night

Celebrate reading on **World Book Night,** every year on 23 April: **worldbooknight.org.uk**

Summer Reading Challenge

Read with your family as part of the **Summer Reading Challenge**: **summerreadingchallenge.org.uk**

For more information on our work and the power of reading visit: **readingagency.org.uk**

More from Quick Reads

If you enjoyed the 2026 Quick Reads, please explore our 6 titles from 2025:

For a complete list of titles and more information on the authors and their books visit: **readingagency.org.uk/quickreads**

First published in Great Britain by Simon & Schuster UK Ltd, 2026

Copyright © Leye Adenle, 2026

The right of Leye Adenle to be identified as author of this work has been
asserted in accordance with the Copyright, Designs and Patents Act, 1988.

1 3 5 7 9 10 8 6 4 2

Simon & Schuster UK Ltd, 1st Floor
222 Gray's Inn Road, London WC1X 8HB

For more than 100 years, Simon & Schuster has championed authors and the
stories they create. By respecting the copyright of an author's intellectual property,
you enable Simon & Schuster and the author to continue publishing exceptional
books for years to come. We thank you for supporting the author's copyright
by purchasing an authorised edition of this book.

No amount of this book may be reproduced or stored in any format, nor may it be
uploaded to any website, database, language-learning model, or other repository,
retrieval, or artificial intelligence system without express permission. All rights
reserved. Enquiries may be directed to Simon & Schuster, 222 Gray's Inn Road,
London WC1X 8HB or RightsMailbox@simonandschuster.co.uk

Simon & Schuster Australia, Sydney
Simon & Schuster India, New Delhi

www.simonandschuster.co.uk
www.simonandschuster.com.au
www.simonandschuster.co.in

The authorised representative in the EEA is Simon & Schuster Netherlands BV,
Herculesplein 96, 3584 AA Utrecht, Netherlands. info@simonandschuster.nl

Simon & Schuster strongly believes in freedom of expression and stands against
censorship in all its forms. For more information, visit BooksBelong.com

A CIP catalogue record for this book is available from the British Library

Paperback ISBN: 978-1-3985-5602-7
eBook ISBN: 978-1-3985-5603-4
Audio ISBN: 978-1-3985-5604-1

This book is a work of fiction. Names, characters, places and incidents are either
a product of the author's imagination or are used fictitiously. Any resemblance
to actual people living or dead, events or locales is entirely coincidental.

Typeset in ITC Stone Serif Std by
Palimpsest Book Production Ltd, Falkirk, Stirlingshire
Printed and Bound in the UK using 100% Renewable Electricity
at CPI Group (UK) Ltd

Bobby Fatokun will return in . . .

FALL FROM GRACE

The first full-length novel in a sharp, timely and darkly funny new private investigator series from a vivid and unforgettable voice in the genre. Perfect for fans of Mick Herron's Zoë Boehm and Robert Galbraith's Cormoran Strike.

SEPTEMBER 2026

SIMON & SCHUSTER

London · New York · Amsterdam/Antwerp · Sydney/Melbourne · Toronto · New Delhi